Eduardo Mendoza is a celebrated Spanish novelist. He won the Premio Planeta prize in 2010 for his novel *Riña de gatos: Madrid, 1936*. His other novels include *The City of Marvels*, *The Year of the Flood* and *The Mystery of the Enchanted Crypt* (also by Telegram). He lives in Barcelona, Spain.

Nick Caistor is former Latin American editor of *Index on Censorship* magazine. His translations include *The Buenos Aires Quintet* by Manuel Vázquez Montalban and works by Eduardo Mendoza, Juan Marsé, Alan Pauls and Guillermo Orsi.

T0162165

Eduardo Mendoza

NO WORD FROM GURB

Translated from Spanish by Nick Caistor

TELEGRAM

First English edition published 2007 by Telegram
This edition published 2013

First published in Spanish in 1991 as *Sin Noticias de Gurb*
by Editorial Seix Barral

ISBN 978 1 84659 016 0

A full CIP record for this book is available
from the British Library.

Printed and bound by Clays Ltd, Elcograf s.p.a.

TELEGRAM
26 Westbourne Grove, London W2 5RH
www.telegrambooks.com

Day 9

00.01 (local time) Landing without problems. Conventional propulsion (amplified). Landing speed: 6.3 on the conventional (restricted) scale. Landing speed: 4 on the Infra-U1 scale, or 9 on the Molina Scale. Cubage: AZ-0.3. Landing area: 63^ (IIb) 284763947836394739374492749. Local name of landing area: Sardanyola.

07.00 Acting on orders (mine), Gurb prepares to make contact with the life forms (real and potential) of the area. Given that we are travelling in non-corporeal form (pure intelligence-analytical factor 4800) decide he should take on a bodily appearance similar to that of local inhabitants. Reason: so as not to attract the attention of the autochthonous fauna (real and potential). Consult the Astral Earth Catalogue of Assimilable Forms (AECAF) and choose to give Gurb the appearance of human being known as Madonna.

07.15 Gurb leaves spaceship through hatch No. 4. Temperature, 15° C; humidity, 56 per cent; clear skies with southerly breeze; seas calm.

07.21 First contact with local inhabitant. Data sent back by Gurb: size of individual specimen, 170 centimetres; diameter of skull, 57 centimetres; number of eyes, 2; length of tail, 0.00 centimetres (missing). Being communicates by means of a language of great structural simplicity, but very complex sound quality, because he has to produce it by means of internal organs. Extremely poor conceptualization. Name of being: Lluc Puig I Roig (impossible to pronounce, due to poor or incomplete reception). Biological function of specimen: tenured professor (sole employment) at Bellaterra Autonomous University. Level of understanding: poor. Has use of a means of transport of great structural simplicity, but great difficulty handling, which goes by name of Ford Fiesta.

07.23 Gurb is invited by being to get into his means of transport. Gurb asks for instructions. Order him to accept. Fundamental objective: not to attract the attention of the autochthonous fauna (real and potential).

07.30 No word from Gurb.

08.00 No word from Gurb.

09.00 No word from Gurb.

12.30 No word from Gurb.

20.30 No word from Gurb.

Day 10

07.00 Decide to set off in search of Gurb. Before leaving, disguise the ship in order to avoid discovery or inspection by autochthonous fauna. Consult Astral Catalogue, and decide to change it into the terrestrial form known as family apartment, spl.lvl, ch, liv.rm. 3beds. 2baths. ktch. sw.pool prem. dblepking. Max. cr.fac.

07.30 Decide to take on appearance of individual human being. Consult Catalogue, and choose his Lordship the Duke of Olivares.

07.45 Leave spaceship via the hatch (now a double door of great structural simplicity but extremely complex handling), choose to materialize in a spot where the concentration of individuals is at its densest. Objective: not to attract attention.

08.00 Materialize at the location known as the Diagonal-Paseo de Gracia crossroads. Knocked down by the No.17 Barceloneta-Vall d'Hebron autobus. Have to recover my head, which has rolled off as a result of collision. Difficult operation due to large number of vehicles.

08.01 Knocked down by Opel Corsa.

08.02 Knocked down by delivery van.

08.03 Knocked down by taxi.

08.04 Recover my head and wash it in a public fountain situated a few metres from collision. Take opportunity to analyse composition of local water: hydrogen, oxygen and faecal matter.

08.15 Given the high concentration of individual specimens, finding Gurb *à l'œil nu* will probably be difficult. Resist temptation to establish sensorial contact, due to lack of knowledge of possible consequences on ecological balance of region and therefore on its inhabitants.

Human beings come in a variety of sizes. The smallest are so small that if other larger ones did not push them in a little vehicle they would quickly be trampled on (and would probably lose their heads). The largest rarely extend more than 200 centimetres.

NB One surprising detail: when they are lying down they are exactly as long as when they are standing up. Some of them have a moustache; others a beard and a moustache; still others a beard, moustache and hair (real or fake). Almost all have two eyes which, depending on how one looks at their heads, are placed either at the front or at the back. In order to walk, they move from backwards to forwards. This means that they have to balance the movement of their legs with a vigorous swinging to and fro of their arms. Those in the greatest hurry reinforce this toing and froing by means of briefcases made of leather or plastic, or small suitcases known as Samsonite, made out of a material from another planet. The means of locomotion of cars (four wheels in parallel, and filled with stale air) is more rational, and allows them to travel at greater speeds. In order not to seem eccentric, am unable to fly or walk on my head. NB Keep one foot (either will do) constantly on the ground, or use the external organ known as arse.

11.00 Will soon have been waiting three hours in the hope of seeing Gurb pass by. Vain wait. The flow of human beings in this part of the city never slackens. Quite the opposite. I calculate the probability of Gurb passing by here without my seeing him at 73 to 1. However, two variables need to be added to this calculation: a) Gurb may not pass by here; b) Gurb may pass by here, but could have modified his external appearance. In the latter case, the probability of my not seeing him would rise to 918 billion to 1.

12.00 Hour of the angelus. Bow head in silent prayer for a few seconds, hoping against hope that Gurb will not pass by at precisely this moment.

13.00 The standing position I have forced my body to adopt for five hours has left me exhausted. Muscular strain plus the continuous effort I have to make to breathe air in and out. I once forgot to do so for more than five minutes. My face turned bright purple; my eyes came out on stalks, and I again had to go and recover them from under the wheels of passing cars. If this goes on, I am going to attract attention to myself. It appears human beings breathe in and out automatically, and call it respiration. This automatic procedure, which cannot help but disgust any civilized creature, and which I am reporting for purely scientific reasons, is something humans employ not merely for respiration, but also for many other bodily functions, such as circulation of the blood, digestion, movement of their eyelids – which unlike the previous two functions, can be controlled, in which case it is known as a wink – growth of fingernails, etc. Human beings are so reliant on the automatic functioning of their organs (and organisms) that they would relieve themselves automatically, too, if they had not been trained from childhood to subordinate nature to decency.

14.00 Reach end of my physical endurance. Rest by putting both knees on the ground, left leg bent backwards, right one bent forwards. Seeing me in this position, old lady offers me a 25-peseta coin, which I immediately swallow so as not to seem rude. Temperature, 20° C; humidity, 64 per cent; slight breeze from south; seas calm.

14.30 Movement on wheels and feet lessens slightly. Still no word from Gurb. At risk of disturbing the planet's delicate ecological balance, decide to establish sensorial contact. Take advantage of a moment when no buses are passing to empty my mind and emit waves on frequency H76420ba1400009, raising this progressively to H76420ba1400010.

At my second attempt, receive signal, at first weak then clearer. Decode message, which is apparently coming from two separate positions, even though they are very close together by comparison to the Earth's diameter. Text of the message (after decoding):

'Where are you calling us from, señora Cargols?'
'From Sant Joan Despi.'
'Where did you say?'
'From Sant Joan Despi. Sant Joan Despi. Can't you hear me?'
'It seems we have a slight technical problem here in the studio, señora Cargols. Can you hear us OK?'
'What was that?'

'I asked if you could hear us all right, señora Cargols?'
'Yes, yes. I can hear you perfectly.'
'Can you hear me, señora Cargols?'
'Yes, fine, fine.'
'So where are you calling us from, señora Cargols?'
'From Sant Joan Despi.'
'From Sant Joan Despi. And you can hear us all right in Sant Joan Despi, señora Cargols?'
'Yes, I can hear you fine. Can you hear me all right?'
'I can hear you fine. Where did you say you were calling from, señora Cargols?'

I begin to fear I may have a lot more difficulty finding Gurb than I at first thought.

15.00 Decide to make a systematic search of the city instead of remaining in one spot. This means the probability of not finding Gurb is reduced tenfold, in other words to 900/18 million, although this still leaves the outcome uncertain. Set off following the ideal heliographic plan I built into my internal circuits on leaving the ship. Fall into a trench dug by the Catalan Gas Company.

15.02 Fall into a trench dug by the Catalan Hydro-electric Company.

15.03 Fall into a trench dug by the Barcelona Water Company.

15.04 Fall into a trench dug by the Calle Corcega Neighbourhood Association.

15.06 Decide to abandon the ideal heliographic plan and to walk watching where I put my feet.

19.00 Walking for four hours now. Have no idea where I am, and my legs can hardly support me any more. The city is huge, and full of people all the time. The noise never stops either. Am surprised not to find the usual monuments, such as the Cenotaph to the Holy Virgin, which I could use as landmarks. Stopped a passer-by who appeared to have a fairly high level of understanding, and asked how I could find a missing person. He asked me how old the person was. When I told him Gurb was 6,513, he suggested I went to look in the Corte Ingles department store. The greatest difficulty comes from having to breathe this atmosphere full of dense particles. It is common knowledge that in certain neighbourhoods the air is so dense that the inhabitants stuff it in skins and export it as black pudding. My eyes are smarting, my nose is blocked, my mouth is dry. Life is better in Sardanyola!

20.30 After sunset, atmospheric conditions would improve considerably if human beings did not insist on lighting the streets. It appears they need to do this in order to be able to stay outside, because it seems that humans – who for the most part have an unfortunate and even ugly appearance – cannot live without constantly seeing each other. Added to this, all the cars have also switched their lights on, in order to attack each other more easily. Temperature, 17° C; relative humidity, 62 per cent; slight breeze from southwest; seas slightly choppy.

21.30 Enough is enough. I cannot take another step. Considerable damage to my physical state. Lost one arm, one leg and both ears. Tongue hanging out so far that after swallowing four dog turds and an unspecified number of cigarette butts have had to tie it to my belt. Better to continue my search tomorrow. Shelter under a stationary lorry, dematerialize, then rematerialize back on board spaceship.

21.45 Recharge my energy sources.

21.50 Get into my pyjamas. Greatly demoralized by Gurb's absence. Having spent all our evenings together for the past 800 years, I've no idea how to kill the time before going to sleep. I could watch local television or read an episode of the *Adventures of Lola Galaxy*, but don't feel like it. Cannot understand Gurb's disappearance, still less his silence. I have never been a demanding boss. I have always allowed my crew – in other words, Gurb – to go out whenever he wanted (in his free time, that is), but if he is planning not to come back, or to come back late, the least he could do is to warn me.

Day 11

08.00 Still no word from Gurb. Try again to establish sensory contact. Hear the angry voice of someone who is demanding, in the name of civic-minded citizens who he claims to represent, that someone by the name of Guerra accept full responsibility. Give up on sensory contact.

08.30 Leave spaceship, take on shape of great crested grebe and survey region from the air.

09.30 Conclude mission and return to ship. The cities are jumbled and irrational in design, but the countryside around them is even worse. Nothing there is straight or flat, as if deliberately made to prevent proper exploitation. And from a bird's eye view, the coastline looks as though it has been drawn by a madman.

09.45 Following a detailed study of a map of Barcelona (cartographic version with double elliptic axis), I decide to continue my search for Gurb in one of the outskirts of the city inhabited by a human variant known as the poor. Since the Astral Catalogue describes them as being slightly less tame than the variant known as the rich, and very much less so than the variant known as the middle class, I decide to take on the appearance of individual being known as Gary Cooper.

10.00 Materialize in an apparently deserted street in the San Cosme neighbourhood. Doubt whether Gurb would have chosen to come here, although he's never exactly been a bright spark.

10.01 A group of adolescents armed with knives steals my saddlebag.

10.02 A group of adolescents armed with knives steals my six-guns and sheriff's badge.

10.03 A group of adolescents armed with knives steals my waistcoat, shirt and trousers.

10.04 A group of adolescents armed with knives steals my boots, spurs and mouth organ.

10.10 A police patrol car pulls up alongside me. A member of the national police gets out, informs me of my constitutional rights, then handcuffs me and throws me into the back of the car. Temperature, 21° C; humidity, 75 per cent; gusts of wind from southerly direction; seas, choppy.

10.30 Placed in police cell. In same cell is a human being of shabby appearance. Introduce myself and tell him the adventures I have met in that dreadful neighbourhood.

10.45 Once the initial suspicion that all members of the human race feel for each other has been overcome, the individual that chance has linked my destiny with decides to strike up a conversation. He hands me his business card:

JETULIO PENCAS
Mendicant salesman
Tarot readings, violin playing, sympathy rousing
Street service or home delivery

10.50 My new friend tells me he's in clink by mistake. He never tried to break into a car, he makes a good and honest living begging and the powders the police took from him are not what they say they are, but the ashes of his deceased father (may the Lord bless and keep him), which he had been intending to spread that very day from up on the Mirador del Alcalde. He goes on to say that all he has just told me, apart from being a pack of lies, is also completely useless, because justice in this country is rotten, and even if there is no evidence or witnesses, just because of the way the two of us look, we are bound to be thrown into jug, from where we will come out riddled with AIDS and fleas. When I say I don't understand any of this, he tells me there is nothing to understand, calls me a real gent and says that's how life is, that the crux of it all is that the rich in this country get away with everything, and it's the poor what gets the blame. He cites as an example the case of an individual whose name I cannot recall who has built himself a chalet with twenty-two privies, adding that he wishes that said individual would get the squits and find they were all occupied. Upon which he stands on the bed in the cell and declares that when his time comes (to use the lavatory?) he will oblige said individual to do his business in the hen-house and will donate the twenty-two privies among twenty-two families on unemployment benefit. That way, he continues, they'll have something to do until they are given a job, as they were promised. At this point, he falls from the bed and splits his head open.

11.30 A member of the national police – different from the previously mentioned individual – opens the cell door and orders us to follow him, apparently for us to appear before the chief inspector. Alerted by my new friend's warnings, I decide to take on a more respectable appearance, and change myself into don

19

José Ortega y Gasset. To show solidarity, I change my new friend into don Miguel de Unamuno.

11.35 We appear before the chief inspector, who looks us over from head to toe, scratches his own head, says he wants a quiet life and orders us to be thrown out into the street.

11.40 My new friend and I say farewell at the door to the police station. Before we part, my new friend begs me to give him back his original appearance, because nobody is going to give him a peseta looking the way he does, not even if he sticks on some artificial pustules that make him look totally revolting. I grant him his wish and he walks away.

11.45 Renew my search.

14.30 Still no word from Gurb. Decide to imitate everyone around me and have lunch. Since all the establishments are shut apart from those called restaurants, deduce this must be where food is served. Sniff in the bins outside several restaurants until I come across one that tickles my fancy.

14.45 Go into the restaurant where a gentleman dressed in black asks me is a surly manner if by any chance I have booked. I reply that I haven't, but that I'm having a chalet built with twenty-two privies in it. Am rushed to a table decorated with a bouquet of flowers, which in order not to appear impolite I immediately consume. Am given the menu (uncoded), read it and order ham, ham and melon, and melon. The gentleman asks what I will have to drink. Not wishing to attract attention, I order the most common human liquid: urine.

16.15 Have a coffee. The house offers me a pear liqueur. Then they bring me my bill: 7,834 pesetas. I don't have a cent.

16.35 Smoke a Montecristo (number two [2]) while I think about how to get out of this tight spot. I could dematerialize, but decide against it because a) this might attract the attention of waiters and the other diners, and b) it would not be fair for such kind people, who have offered me this pear liqueur, to have to suffer the consequences of my own foolishness.

16.40 Excuse myself, saying that I have forgotten something in the car. Leave the restaurant, go into a newsagent, and buy coupons and tickets for all the huge variety of lotteries on offer.

16.45 Using elementary calculus to manipulate the numbers, win the amount of 122,000,000 pesetas. Return to the restaurant, pay my bill and leave a hundred million tip.

16.55 Renew my search for Gurb in the only way I know: pounding the streets.

20.00 Walked so much my shoes start smoking. Heel has come off one shoe, which gives my walk a ridiculous mincing effect. Throw shoes away, go into a shop and with the money left over from the restaurant buy a new pair. They are not as comfortable as the previous ones, but are made of very tough material. Wearing these new shoes, known here as skis, I start to explore the neighbourhood known as Pedralbes.

21.00 Finish my exploration of the Pedralbes neighbourhood. Have not found Gurb, but am very favourably impressed by the elegance of Pedralbes's houses, the quiet charm of its streets, the carefully trimmed lawns and its full swimming pools. Have no idea why some people prefer to live in neighbourhoods like San Cosme when they could live in Padralbes. Perhaps it is not so much to do with choice as with money.

Amongst other categories, human beings are apparently divided into rich and poor. This is a division to which they attach huge importance, without knowing why. The fundamental difference between rich and poor seems to be this: the rich, wherever they go, do not pay, even though they acquire or consume as much as they like. The poor, on the other hand, pay through the nose. This exemption enjoyed by the rich can be a matter of tradition or have been recently acquired, or be temporary, or even a sham; this apparently does not matter. From a statistical point of view, it seems clear that the rich live longer and better than the poor, are taller, healthier and better looking, have more fun, travel to more exotic locations, receive better education, work less, are surrounded by more luxuries, have more clothes (especially those of mid-season) and better health care, are buried with greater ceremony and are remembered longer. They are also more likely to appear in newspapers, magazines and annuals.

21.30 Decide to return to spaceship. Dematerialize outside the front door of the Pedralbes convent, to the astonishment of the reverend mother, who is putting out the rubbish at that very moment.

22.00 Recharge energy. Prepare for another lonely evening. Read a chapter of *Lola Galaxy*, but as this is something I have so often done with Gurb – who I always have to explain the hot bits to, because there's no one more naive than him – it makes me sad rather than happy.

22.30 Fed up with wandering around the empty ship, decide to go to bed. Today has been a very tiring day. Put on my pyjamas, say my prayers and lie down.

Day 12

08.00 Still no word from Gurb. Pouring with rain. In Barcelona it rains the way the City Council acts: seldom but like billy-o. Decide not to leave the ship and use the morning to do the housework.

09.00 Cleaning for an hour now, and can't bear it any more. I have always got Gurb to do this sort of thing, so now I'm completely out of training. I hope to God he comes back soon.

09.10 To kill time, decide to watch TV. Various individuals appear, apparently belonging to human race. After some time watching them I realize that I'm seeing a competition like the ones that are so popular on my planet, although the content here is much less elaborate. A couple with biologically different sexes (though this is not immediately visible) are asked what Napoleon's family name was. Whispering all round. The woman answers hesitatingly: Benavente? Wrong answer. Now it's the turn of the rival couple, who are standing on a podium at the opposite side of the studio. Bombita? Wrong again. The presenter applauds, and tells the contestants that they have lost or won 500,000 pesetas. Uproar on the respective podiums. A new contestant enters the fray: she has been on the programme for the past twenty-two months. She is asked what Pedro Almodovar's maiden name was. I decide to switch off. Temperature, 16º C; humidity, 90 per cent; strong northwesterly winds; seas, rough.

09.55 In the shape of Cary Grant (with spectacles) I materialize in the local bar, where I order pair of eggs and bacon and scan the morning papers. Human beings have such a primitive conceptual system that to find out what is going on they have to read the papers. They do not realize that a simple hen's egg contains far more information than all the country's papers put together. And it's more reliable. In the two I have just been served, for example, despite the layers of grease, I can see the stock exchange prices, an opinion poll about politicians' honesty (some 70 per cent of hens consider that politicians are honest) and the result of tomorrow night's basketball games. How easy life would be for human beings if only they had been taught to decipher such things!

10.30 The coffee with brandy worked a treat. Return to the spaceship, put on my pyjamas and lie down. Decide to devote the rest of the day to having a rest. In order not to waste time, decide to embark on a systematic exploration of contemporary Spanish narrative, so highly regarded on this and many other planets.

13.30 Finish reading *Bertoldo, Bertoldino and Cacaseno*. It has stopped raining, but the sky is still cloudy. I decide to go into town. I want to sort out the money question once and for all. I still have some left from yesterday's lottery, but I'd prefer to make sure I lead a comfortable existence for however long my stay on Earth lasts.

13.50 Ten minutes before it closes, I appear at the Sierra Morena Savings Bank. Ask to open an account. In order to inspire confidence, I have taken on the appearance of His Holiness Pope Pius XII, of fond memory.

13.52 The counter clerk hands me a form, which I fill in.

13.55 The counter clerk smiles and informs me that his institution offers a wide variety of accounts (deposit account, composite account, gone-with-the-wind account, pull-the-other-one account, small-print-takes-it-away account). If my investment is above a certain amount, one or other of these facilities will offer me greater profitability, availability or more fiscal opportunities, he says. Reply that I would like to open an account with 22 pesetas.

13.57 The counter clerk stops smiling, stops giving me information and, if my ears do not deceive me, passes wind very loudly. After which, he starts to type on a computer.

13.59 My current account has been opened. At one second to the close of business for the day, give instructions to the computer to add fourteen zeros to my account balance. All done. I leave the bank. It looks as though the sun is trying to come out.

14.30 Stop outside a seafood bar. I know that human beings are in the habit of celebrating a successful business transaction in this kind of place, and I would like to do the same. Seafood bars are a variety or category of restaurant that have the following characteristics: a) they are decorated with all kinds of fishing tackle (this is their most important feature), and b) in them one can ingest a kind of telephone with legs, as well as other animals that offend the senses of taste, sight and smell in equal measure.

14.45 After hesitating for a while (fifteen minutes), and considering the fact that I hate eating alone, I decide to postpone the seafood bar ceremony until I meet up with Gurb. Then, before I apply the necessary sanctions for his misconduct, we can celebrate our re-encounter with a blowout.

15.00 Now that I have money, I decide to visit the city centre and its famous stores. The sky has clouded over again, but for the moment it seems as though the weather will hold.

16.00 Go into a boutique. Buy myself a tie. Try it on. Decide it looks good, so I buy ninety-four more of the same.

16.30 Go into a sports goods shop. Buy a torch, canteen and gas stove for camping. A Barcelona football Club shirt, a tennis racquet, a complete set of windsurf gear (phosphorescent pink) and thirty pairs of trainers.

17.00 Go into a pork butcher's and buy 700 *pata negra* hams.

17.20 Go into a car salesroom and buy a Maserati.

17.45 Go into an electrical goods store and buy everything.

18.00 Go into a toyshop and buy an Indian mask, 112 Barbie dolls and a spinning-top.

18.30 Go into a wine cellar and buy five bottles of Chateau Baron Mouchoir Moqué '52, and a demijohn of El Pentateuco table wine.

19.00 Go into a jeweller's and buy an automatic, waterproof, anti-magnetic and shock-resistant gold Rolex. Smash it on the spot.

19.30 Go into a pharmacist's and buy fifteen bottles of Eau de Ferum perfume, which has just been launched.

20.00 Decide that money cannot buy happiness, so zap everything I have bought and walk with hands in pockets, free as a bird.

20.40 As I go down the Ramblas, the sky grows dark and there is the sound of thunder: obviously, an electrical storm is closing in.

20.42 Due to this damned radioactivity of mine, am struck three times by lightning. My belt buckle and my trouser zip melt. All my hair stands on end, and there is no way to control it: I look like a porcupine.

20.50 Still full of static electricity, try to buy *Leisure Guide* but set fire to the news-stand.

21.03 Three or four drops of rain fall, and just when it seems that might be it, there is such an almighty downpour that the rats rush out of the sewers and climb Columbus's Column just in case. Run to a near-by bar for shelter.

21.04 In the bar. Various kinds of sausage and other stalactites drop grease onto the locals, namely seven or eight individuals with biologically different sexes (although this is not immediately visible except in the case of a gentleman who comes out of the toilet without remembering to put away his willy). Behind the bar wine is being served by what at first I take to be a man. Closer examination reveals that in fact it is two dwarves, one standing on the other's shoulders. Whenever the door opens, the draught drives away the flies. This means that the surface of the mirror appears along one of the walls: in its top right-hand corner written in chalk are the results of the football matches played on 5 March 1958.

21.10 Soaked to the skin by the downpour, I order a glass of red to warm me up. Try to stab one of the appetizers, but to my astonishment it and all the others scurry off along the bar.

21.30 Amuse myself by listening to the locals' conversation. Without decoding, the language human beings use is laborious and childish. To them, an elementary sentence such as: 109328745108and34-19 'poe8vhqa9enf087qjnrf-09aqsdnfñ9q8w3r421dfkf=q

3wyoiqwe=q3u lo9=853491926rn 1nfp2485 1ir0934 8413k8449f385j9t830t82=34utt2egu-34851mfkfg – 2311fgklwhgq0i2ui34756=13ir2487-2349r20i45u62- 4852ut-34582-9238v43 597 46 82=3t98458 9672394ut945467=2-3tugywoit =238tej 93 46 7523 fiwu6-23f3yt-238984rohg-2343ijn87b8b7ytgyt65- 4376687by79 (give me 9 kilos of turnips) is incomprehensible. They therefore talk at great length and in very loud voices, with lots of gestures and horrible grimaces. Even so, their range of expressions is very limited, except when it comes to blaspheming or obscenities, and in their expressions they often employ amphibology, anacoluthons and polysemies.

21.50 While considering this, the waiter keeps topping up my glass, so that before I realize it I've drunk half a litre of the red stuff. I start to analyse the chemical composition of the wine (106 components, none of them derived from grapes) but when I reach trinitrotoluene, I desist. The waiter refills my glass.

22.00 Burst out giggling for no reason, and the individual standing next to me asks who I'm looking at. I explain I'm not laughing at him, but at a silly idea that has just crossed my mind without my knowing why. As my explanation is somewhat confused, especially as I forget to decode some of it, all the locals' eyes turn in my direction.

22.05 One of the locals (not the one who wants to know who I'm looking at) sticks his right forefinger on the end of my nose and says my face looks familiar. The fact that he has recognized me in the guise (and body) of the Holy Father tells me he must be a very devout person, and therefore completely trustworthy. I tell him he must have been mistaken, and to take his and everyone else's attention off me, I offer to buy everyone a round. Seeing me willing to spend money, the waiter says there is tripe fresh from the oven, finger-lickin' good, he says. Place some notes on the bar (5,000,000 pesetas) and say I'll have some of that, money is no problem.

22.12 The devout local says no way, I've already paid for the wine and he'll get in the tripe. The least he can do, he says. I insist the tripe was my idea, and that therefore I should pay for it.

22.17 A woman (also a local), who has just drained her second bottle of absinthe, comes over and tells us it's not worth arguing about. She sticks her hand down her front and pulls out a bundle of dirty, crumpled banknotes. She throws them on the counter. Another local thinks they must be the tripe and eats a mouthful of them. The woman insists it's on her. The devout local says there's no way a woman is going to buy him anything. He says he's a man with balls.

22.24 The tripe has still not appeared, so I bang on the counter with an ashtray. Smash the ashtray and crack the counter. The waiter serves more wine. One of the locals who until now has not spoken says he would like to offer us some wee laments. With great emotion he sings the song entitled 1092387nqfp983j41093 ('Come back to me, bitch') while we all clap our hands, stamp our feet and shout *olé, olé* (7v5,7v5). The pious local says he's finally remembered who I am: Captain Haddock.

22.41 (approximately) The mellifluous local opens his mouth so wide to pour out his sorrows that his false teeth drop into the dish of meatballs. When he puts his hand in to recover them, the waiter hits him on the head with an Edam and tells him that's enough, that he's already snitched eight meatballs that week with the same old trick, but that he's no (incomprehensible) and knows how many there are in there. The rebuked songster replies that he has no need to steal meatballs from a dump like this, that he was once king of the Spanish copla in Paris, and that he has his own table whenever he likes at Maxim's. The waiter's only response is to serve more wine.

23.00 The asshole who wanted to know who I was looking at tells us that he could have been someone, because he has always had ideas and the gumption to put them into practice, but three things have prevented him from doing so, namely: a) bad luck, b) his weakness for a tipple, gambling and women, and c) the hatred of some powerful people he prefers not to name. The old tart who earlier fished the dough out of her bristols leaps up and says hang on a minute, the real reasons you have never got anywhere are: a) laziness, b) laziness, c) laziness. She says she's fed up to the back teeth of having to listen to all this stuff and nonsense.

? The tripe finally comes walking out of the kitchen under its own steam. The slag says she is the only one among them who has anything to be proud of, because until recently she was a high-class whore, known in her neighbourhood as the Oklahoma Bombshell. To this she adds that if she looks a little the worse for wear, it's not because of her age, but for other reasons, such as a) her passion for dried beans, b) the beatings her men have given her, and c) the botched cosmetic surgery a surgeon whose name she prefers to forget gave her for free. At this she bursts into tears. So I go and tell her not to cry, that to me she is the most beautiful and attractive woman I have ever seen, and that I would gladly marry her, but am unable to due to the fact that I am an extraterrestrial and am just passing through on the way to another galaxy, to which she replies that they all say that. The cretin who wanted to know who I was looking at tells her to stop talking (incomprehensible) and to shut up, to which she replies (touché!) that no son of a (incomprehensible) is going to tell her to be quiet, she will say whatever comes into her noggin and what of it. So I go and punch the guy who has insulted her in the mouth. I tell him where to (incomprehensible) or possibly I punch somebody else, but it doesn't matter, because I tell the lot of them straight out that no one is going to insult my fiancée like that.

Darkest night. The guy I knocked down gets up from the floor, seizes me by the ears and whirls me round like a ceiling fan. Taking advantage of the confusion, the songster stuffs a handful of meatballs in his mouth. The waiter hits him in the stomach with a frying pan and forces him to return the meatballs (or something similar) to the original dish. The national police come in brandishing truncheons. I manage to wrench the truncheon from one of their hands and use it to beat another (or possibly the same) policeman over the head with. Things seem to be getting rather complicated. I decide to dematerialize, but get the formula wrong and zap two snack bars on the Moll de la Fusta. We are all taken to the police station.

Day 13

08.00 Hauled before the chief inspector. The chief inspector notifies me that all my drinking companions have given their statements while I was sleeping like a log, and that all of them agree I was the cause of all the trouble. Having thus proven their innocence, they have all been released. By this time they must all be back in the bar, having completely forgotten about me. I feel so abandoned that without wishing or meaning to I am transformed into Paquirrín the bullfighter. The chief inspector cautions me, then tells his men to throw me out. How ashamed I feel! And what a hangover!

08.45 Return to the ship. No message on the answering machine. Recharge energy, put on pyjamas.

13.00 Wake up, feeling much better. Frugal breakfast. Decide not to eat today. Read one after the other

Tontolina on Holiday, Tontolina at School and *Tontolina Comes Out.*

15.00 Power failure. Something is wrong in the ship's generators. Go to the engine room to see if I can identify the fault. Press buttons and move levers to see if by some miracle this sorts the problem out, because I don't understand a thing about machinery. Gurb was always the one who made everything work, or repaired this crap when it broke down. Discover several leaks, listed on the attached sheet.

16.00 Must have touched something I shouldn't have, because the spaceship has been filled with an unbearable stench. Step outside and realize that by mistake I have inverted the functioning of one of the turbines. Instead of expelling the energy produced by the breakdown of cadmium and plutonium, the turbine is sucking up the village sewage system.

16.10 Take on the appearance (and virtues) of Admiral Yamamoto and try to bale out the ship with a bucket.

16.15 Give up.

16.17 Leave the ship. Just in case Gurb comes back during my absence, leave this note pinned to the door: 'Gurb, have been forced to abandon ship (honourably); if you come back, leave a message saying where I can find you at the village bar (señor Joaquín or señora Mercedes).'

16.40 Appear in the village bar. Tell señora Mercedes (señor Joaquín is taking his siesta) that if a being of any shape or size, or a being without any shape or size at all, should ask for me, could she please take a message. I'll be back when I can. What more can I do?

17.23 Transfer to city on public transport called City Railway. Unlike other living organisms (the dung beetle, for example), which always move around in the same way, human beings use a great variety of means of transport, all of which compete to see which can be the slowest, most uncomfortable and most smelly – although the winners in this last category are usually feet or certain taxis. The wrongly named metro is the means of transport smokers prefer; the bus is the transport of choice for those people, usually elderly, who like to turn somersaults in the air. For longer distances there are the so-called aeroplanes, a sort of bus that travels forward by expelling air from its tyres. This enables it to reach the lower levels of the atmosphere, where it stays up thanks to the intervention of the saint whose name is written on its fuselage (Saint Teresa of Avila, Saint Ignatius Loyola, and so on). On long journeys, the passengers in these aeroplanes pass the time showing each other their socks.

18.30 Need to find somewhere to stay the night, because there is no guarantee there will not be another downpour like yesterday, or even hail. Besides which, even if the sky stays clear, my experience of the streets in Barcelona has taught me that it is very unwise to spend any longer than is strictly necessary on them.

19.30 Have been going from hotel to hotel for an hour now. There is not a single room free in the entire city, because, as I have been told, there is a symposium on New Ways to Stuff Piquillo Peppers, attended by experts from all over the world.

20.30 Another hour's search and increasing experience of how to give tips enables me to secure an en-suite bedroom with a view of a sizeable public works building site. With the aid of a megaphone, the receptionist informs me that the drilling and demolition work will stop at night.

21.30 At an outlet close to the hotel I order and consume a burger. This is a composite of bits and pieces from a wide range of animals. A rapid analysis allows me to detect ox, ass, dromedary, elephant (Asian and African), mandril, gnu and fossilized megatherium. I also find tiny amounts of bluebottles and dragonflies, half a badminton racquet, two screws, a cork and a certain amount of gravel. I wash down my meal with a large bottle of Zumifot.

22.20 Take a stroll back to the hotel. A warm, perfumed night. Temperature, 21º C; humidity, 63 per cent; gentle breeze; seas, calm. Go into the hotel bar in search of company. Only human being present is the barman, gargling in the cocktail shaker. Ask for my key and retire.

22.30 Put on my pyjamas. Watch Catalan television for a short while.

22.50 Get into bed. Read the memoirs of don Soponcio Velludo: *Forty Years as Land Surveyor in Albacete*.

24.00 Work outside ceases. Say my prayers and switch off the light. Still no word from Gurb.

02.27 For no apparent reason, minibar explodes. Spend half an hour picking up all the plastic bottles.

03.01 The works outside have caused a gas leak. All the hotel guests are evacuated via the fire escape.

04.00 Gas leak repaired. All hotel guests allowed to return to their rooms.

04.53 Fire in the hotel kitchens. All hotel guests evacuated via the main staircase, as the fire escape is enveloped in flames.

05.19 Arrival of the fire brigade. They put out the blaze instantly. All hotel guests return to their respective rooms.

06.00 The diggers start up.

06.05 I pay my hotel bill and leave my room. It is immediately taken by a travelling food salesman who has spent the night in the open. He tells me that the firm he represents has succeeded in creating boneless chickens, which are greatly appreciated at the dinner table, but a bit floppy while alive.

Day 14

07.00 Appear at señora Mercedes and señor Joaquín's bar just as señora Mercedes is raising the metal shutter. Help her take down the chairs that señor Joaquín put up on the tables the previous night to make sweeping the floor easier. She tells me that nobody has asked for me. Beg her to keep her eyes peeled. She makes me an aubergine omelette (my favourite), which I eat with two slices of bread smeared with tomato and a beer, while I glance at the morning papers. It seems the team for Italy has already been chosen: Zubizarreta, Chendo, Alkorta, Sanchis, Rafa Paz, Villaroya, Michel, Martín Vázquez, Roberto Salinas, Butragueño, Bakero. What a team! Carefully study the small ads to see if I can find an apartment to rent. Easier said than done. Better to buy.

09.30 Appear at an estate agent's. In order to create a good impression, have adopted the shape of the Duke and Duchess of Kent. Am taken to a room where several people are already waiting.

09.50 Read extensive coverage of the wedding of someone called Baudouin and Fabiola in a copy of *Hello!* Realize this must be an old issue.

10.00 A young lady comes in and divides us into three groups: a) those who want to purchase an apartment to live in, b) those who want to purchase an apartment for money-laundering purposes, and c) those who want to purchase an apartment in the Olympic Village. A couple with a babe in arms and myself make up Group A.

10.15 We members of Group A are led into a gloomy office. A gentleman with a white beard is seated at a desk, the picture of honesty. He explains that this is a difficult moment, that there is more demand than supply and vice versa, that we should not get our hopes up. He urges us to forget about the deceptive quality-price nexus. He reminds us that this life is nothing but a vale of tears with all mod cons. Halfway through his sermon his fake beard peels off. He throws it in the bin.

11.25 Visit the apartment I have just bought. Not bad. I'll have to put in a kitchen and bathrooms, but that does not worry me, as I don't know how to cook and never wash. Delighted to see that the bedroom has a spacious wardrobe set in the wall. Get inside the wardrobe and it starts to move. Disappointment: it's the lift.

14.50 Obtain municipal permit, sign on for water, gas, electricity and telephone, take out insurance for fire and theft, pay the council tax.

16.30 Buy a bed, a sofa bed (for guests), a three-piece suite, sideboard, table and chairs. Temperature, 21° C; humidity, 60 per cent; light winds; seas, choppy.

17.58 Buy cutlery and crockery.

18.20 Buy linen and curtains.

19.00 Buy vacuum cleaner, microwave oven, steam iron, toaster, frying pan, hairdryer.

19.30 Buy detergent, fabric softener, polish, window cream, broom, floor cloth, scourer, chamois leather.

20.30 Settle down at home. Get a takeaway pizza and a family-size bottle of Zumifot. Put on my pyjamas.

21.30 Decide to abandon (just for today) my reading list of Spanish narratives and go to bed with a thriller by an English woman writer held in high esteem by human beings. The plot of her novel is very simple. An individual who, to simplify, we will call A, is found dead in the library. Another individual, B, tries to discover who killed A and why. Following a series of illogical undertakings (all that was needed was the formula $3(x2-r)n-+0$ and the case would have been solved from the start), B states (wrongly) that the murderer is C. Everyone seems happy with this conclusion, including C. No idea what a butler is.

01.30 Say my prayers and get ready for bed. Still no word from Gurb.

04.17 Wake up and cannot get back to sleep. Get up and roam my new apartment. Something is missing, but I'm not sure what.

05.40 Overcome with tiredness, fall back to sleep without having resolved the mystery tormenting me.

06.11 Wake up with a start. Know what's missing to make the apartment a true home. But will I find a woman willing to share my life with me?

Day 15

07.00 Help señora Mercedes raise the metal shutter on the bar and plug in the coffee machine. Señor Joaquín is dead to the world. He drives señora Mercedes nuts. She stresses the difference between señor Joaquín, whom she calls a slob, and a man like me, up early in the morning, hard-working and polite with it. I ask if in her opinion I would find it hard to get a girlfriend. She asks if my intentions are serious, or if I just want a bit of fun. I protest that I am completely serious. She says that if that is the case I will have girls in droves. She says I'll have to study the form. To change the topic, I ask her if there has been any message for me, and she replies in the affirmative. My heart skips a beat. Could this be a word from Gurb?

09.15 Señora Mercedes brings me my aubergine omelette, my beer and a coded message. Disappointment: it's not from Gurb but from the Supreme Board of Space Research, based on Space Station AF, in the constellation of Antares. Decide to leave the message for later, eat my omelette and drink my beer.

09.30 A little burp.

09.35 Lock myself in the men's toilet to read the message in peace.

09.55 Having some difficulty deciphering the message. Another client in a hurry hammers on the toilet door.

10.40 Message decoded. The Supreme Board wants to know why the Spanish manager did not pick Mickey Mouse. Impossible to reply without my encoding machine, which I left in the spaceship.

11.00 Return home on the metro. On the way, study the girls getting on and off. Choosing one among so many will be no easy matter, because that will mean giving up the others, and almost all of them are gorgeous.

13.00 Decide to spend the afternoon studying the question.

15.00 For methodological reasons, decide to divide the problem into three groups or categories: a) biological difficulties, b) psychological difficulties, c) practical difficulties. All three seem to me insurmountable.

15.30 A few useful details: the reproductive organs of human beings are divided into two, known respectively as upstairs and downstairs. The latter has an appendage or peduncle known as willy.

17.05 Go down to newsagent and buy the Playboy calendar. Run back up to apartment, hiding the calendar under my sports jacket.

17.15 Wonder whether the peculiar anatomy of the ladies photographed in the calendar would allow them to withstand a pressure of 90,000 atmospheres.

19.00 Spend a large part of the afternoon investigating the matter in hand. Question: when should a gentleman show respect for a lady? Answer: when her moral qualities, her social condition, her modesty in dress and her personal hygiene have shown she merits it. Should this not be so, the use of violence is optional. Other details I need to memorize: when should flowers be sent or not sent to a funeral? When can one get personal? Hat, gloves and a cane. Faced with the baptismal font, a difficult moment. Appetizers, canapés and petits fours. Poise at all times!

20.00 Rehearse some possible human forms in front of the mirror. Women are conquered by the eyes; the first impression is vital. Quasimodo, Papa Hemngway, Giorgio Armani, Eisenhower.

20.30 Decide to go for a walk to clear my head. Temperature, 18° C; humidity, 65 per cent; moderate breeze; seas, calm.

20.55 Few cities on Earth can pride themselves on having such a wide variety of cultural attractions as Barcelona. Unfortunately, the timing of these events does not always fit in with its inhabitants' lives. For example, the whale orca only performs at specific times in the mornings; and so on and so forth. Fortunately, my steps have led me to the Ramblas just as a performance at the Liceo opera house is about to begin.

23.30 The Liceo is undoubtedly the leading opera house in Spain, and one of the foremost in Europe. However, it suffers from an endemic financial crisis, which means that the musical events it puts on are not always of the highest quality. Tonight, as the programme baldly states, the resident orchestra and choirs could not make up their numbers. Instead, the barber-shop group from the Faculty of Engineering did its best, but *Boris Godunov* sounded rather flat.

24.00 Return home. Still no word from Gurb. Pyjamas, teeth, little Jesus meek and mild, shut-eye.

Day 16

07.00 Help señor Joaquín raise the metal shutter and put out the chairs. Distribute the serviette boxes on the bar, with some semi-transparent cylinders containing toothpicks, which can be removed (not without difficulty) through a small hole in the top of the apparatus. While I am working, I enquire after señora Mercedes, who I am surprised not to see at her post. Señor Joaquín tells me that his wife, also known as señora Mercedes, has had a night and a half, and has gone to the clinic first thing. He is afraid she has got another stone. I say a prayer for her total and speedy recovery. Today, instead of aubergine omelette I get bread and tomato and cold sausage. I ask: is there any message for me? No, there are no messages for me.

09.00 Glance through the morning papers and discuss them with the customers who arrive. General concern over the dispute between the municipalities of Salou and

Vilaseca. One elderly customer remembers the sadly notorious Danzig Corridor and all that led to. Another points out that the mere fact that there are nuclear weapons means open war is unthinkable, despite the angry tone both municipalities have adopted. A further thought: people are dumb. Another one: the devil makes work for idle hands. Some useful words: silversmith's anvil, trivet; people from the Canary Islands, canaries.

09.10 Señora Mercedes arrives in a taxi, pale but with a smile on her face. She has to have X-rays tomorrow, but the diagnosis is optimistic: just a few granules. She wants immediately to start washing up, but we forbid her. What she needs is rest, rest and more rest. I put on her apron and scrub plates, cups and glasses. Break two.

11.00 Visit the works being carried out for the Olympic Ring, the National Palace and the Outer Circular Avenue. I detect a certain unease among some sectors of public opinion, because they say the cost will be much higher than first budgeted for. The same cannot be said for income. Human beings have not learned to build the time factor into their calculations, with the result that, whatever they say, they are worse than useless. It would be easy enough for them to correct their mistake, if only they were aware of it. As of now, however, they are incapable of understanding even a simple problem, such as: if a pear is worth 3 pesetas now, how much will three pears be worth in the year

3628? Answer: 987,365,409,587,635,294,736,489 pesetas. Moreover, the debate, applied to the Olympic Ring, is meaningless, because before the year 2000 all the Central Banks will have gone off the gold standard and adopted the three varieties of Elgorriaga chocolate: milk, dark or with hazelnuts.

15.00 Fried fish in Barceloneta. Whisky cake, coffee, Farias cigar. Then home. Alka-Seltzer.

19.30 Wake from my siesta in time to see the basket-ball semi-final on TV2. Barcelona plays badly – the players seem unsettled, but they win by a whisker in the last minute. Give thanks to God. Temperature, 22° C; humidity, 75 per cent; clear skies; light southerly winds; seas, calm.

23.00 Go on a bar crawl to try my luck. If the opportunity arises, I don't intend to miss it. Before leaving take on the appearance of the matador Frascuelo Junior. If it's style they want, they'll get it.

23.30 Crème de menthe in fashionable bar, Bonanova; FAD interior design award winner. Only a few girls, all with partners.

00.00 Crème de menthe in a fashionable bar, Ensanche; FAD interior design award winner. Quite a few girls, all with partners.

00.30 Crème de menthe in fashionable bar, Raval; FAD interior design award winner (first equal). Lots of girls; all with partners.

01.00 Crème de menthe in fashionable bar, Pueblo Nuevo; FAD urban restoration award winner. No girls: must have got the wrong place.

01.30 Crème de menthe in fashionable bar, Sants; finalist in FAD interior design competition. Girls on their own, but expensive.

02.00 Crème de menthe in fashionable bar, Hospitalet; no awards. Lots of girls on their own. Cool atmosphere. Live music. Go up on stage, grab the mike and start singing. My own composition, especially written for the occasion. It goes like this:

Get it on, man
Get it on, man
Get it on, man
Get it on, man
Get it on, man
If you want to get it on
Get it on, man
(chorus)
Get it on, man
Get it on, man (etc)

Sense that they like it, so repeat the song several times. Various heavily built individuals climb on stage and invite me to leave the building. In this past week I have already had two run-ins with the police, so accept their kind invitation.

04.21 Vomit in a flowerbed in the Plaza Urquinaona.

04.26 Vomit in a flowerbed in the Plaza Cataluña.

04.32 Vomit in a flowerbed in the Plaza Universidad.

04.40 Vomit in the pedestrian subway at the intersection of Muntaner and Aragón.

04.50 Stop a taxi and ask him to take me home. Vomit in the taxi.

Day 17

11.30 Wake up in my bed. No idea how I got here. I still have my matador's jacket on, but I've lost my hat, the sword and a bull's ear I won for my prowess, I think. Try to get up, but fail. I won't even mention my head. I decide to stay in bed, taking it easy. Besides, today is Sunday and señora Mercedes and señor Joaquín's bar will be closed. Still no word from Gurb.

14.00 Get dressed and go out for a walk. The weather is hot and there are few people on the street. Many families have gone to spend the weekend in the countryside, in their second homes. Everything is bolted and barred: the shops, of course, but also the bars and restaurants. I couldn't care less: the way my stomach feels, I couldn't eat a thing.

14.20 Find a small sports goods shop that on normal days doesn't sell as much as a hatpin. Possibly this is why they open on Sundays and hire bicycles. Rent a bike. It's a very simply conceived apparatus but very difficult handling because it requires the simultaneous use of *both* legs, unlike walking, which allows you to leave one leg unused while the other moves forwards. This gesture or part of a gesture (depending on how you look at it) is known as taking a step. If in walking the left foot is placed to the right of the right foot and then, in the next gesture or part of a gesture, the opposite takes place, in other words the right foot is placed to the left of the left foot, this is known as a mincing step.

15.00 As the street has a pronounced incline, riding a bicycle has two distinct parts to it, i.e. a) going down, b) going up. The first part (going down) is delightful; the second (going up) is torture. Fortunately, bicycles have brakes placed on each end of their handlebars. When these brakes are applied, they prevent the bicycle acquiring an increasing or dangerous speed in any descent. In climbs, the brakes prevent the bicycle from rolling backwards.

17.30 Return the bicycle. The exercise has awakened my appetite. Find a baker's open and eat a kilo of churros, a kilo and a half of buns and three kilos of pancakes.

18.00 Sit on a bench in the street to help digest the food. The traffic, which until now was practically non-existent, is growing heavier by the minute. This is because everyone is returning to the city. On the access routes to the city there are many hold-ups, which often become important hold-ups. Some of these, especially the important hold-ups, last until the following weekend, so that some unfortunate people (including entire families) spend their lives travelling from the countryside to the hold-ups and then from the hold-ups back to the country, without ever being able to reach the city they live in – causing severe problems for their family economy and their children's schooling.

The density of the road traffic is one of this city's most serious problems, and one of the things that most concerns the mayor, also known as Maragall. He has on several occasions recommended the use of bicycles instead, and has appeared in the press sitting on one of these contraptions (although to tell the truth it does not seem as though he has travelled very far on it). Perhaps people would make more use of the bicycle if the city were less hilly, but this would be difficult to achieve, as almost all the hills have been built on. Another solution would be for City Hall to provide bicycles for the use of those living at the tops of the hills, so that they could use them to get to the centre very quickly and almost without having to pedal. Once the bikes were in the centre, the authorities (or even a sub-contractor) could load them onto trucks and take them back up to the tops of the hills. This system would be relatively cheap. At most, the authorities would need to place a net or some kind of mattress at the bottoms of the hills to prevent the less expert or crazier cyclists from falling into the Mediterranean at the ends of their descents. This would not of course solve the problem of how those people who had come down to the centre on their bikes would get back up to their homes, but this is not something that should worry City Hall, because it is not part of the duties of that institution (or any other) to limit any citizen's sense of initiative. Another invention: a chemical product and an ignition mechanism that would allow one to light cigars just by pressing the cigar band. Temperature, 21° C; humidity, 75 per cent; moderate breeze; seas, calm.

19.10 Return home. In the doorway meet the lady from the third floor with her son. They've left their car double parked while she unloads bags and packages. She refuses my offer of help. Tells me it's the same pain in the neck every weekend, and that she is used to it. I insist, and she allows me to carry a plastic bag full of sausages. Ask her if she made them herself. Reply: no, I bought them in a little village near La Bisbal, where I have a house. Question: so why do you bring them here to eat? Reply: I don't understand the question.

19.25 Once the unloading and transfer of bags and packages from the car to the lift is complete, we get into the lift. Take advantage of my neighbour's proximity to calibrate her physical measurements. Height of my neighbour (standing), 173 centimetres; length of longest hair (top of head), 47 centimetres; shortest (upper lip), 0.002 centimetres; distance from elbow to fingernail (thumb), 40 centimetres; distance from left elbow to right elbow, 36 centimetres (standing to attention), 126 centimetres (hands on hips).

19.26 We take bags and packages out of the lift and place them on the third-floor landing. My neighbour thanks me for my help and says she would invite me in, but her boy is exhausted. He has to have a bath, eat and then go straight to bed, because he's got school in the morning. I say I don't want to put her to any trouble, and besides, we'll see each other again because I live in the same building. My neighbour tells me she already knew that, because the caretaker had told her about me. Could she have mentioned my dissolute habits?

20.00 So caught up with my neighbour, only get to eight o'clock Mass by miracle. Lengthy but interesting sermon. Put not your trust in those who seek to fool you, but rather in those who do *not* seek to fool you.

21.30 Reach the baker's just as they are about to shut. Buy all the churros they have left.

22.00 Eat everything I've bought watching the TV. I definitely like my neighbour. Sometimes we roam the universe for what is on our own doorstep. This often happens to us astronauts.

23.00 Pyjamas, teeth. What about buying a motor-bike?

23.15 Read *Half a Century of Hairdressing in Spain* (Vol. I, Republic and Civil War).

00.30 Prayers. Still no word from Gurb.

Day 18

07.00 Appear at señora Mercedes and señor Joaquín's bar and find both of them – that is, señora Mercedes and señor Joaquín – *closing* the metal shutter. What can be the reason for this change in habits? Or rather, what can be the reason for this *reversal* of habits? Explanation: señora Mercedes has had another night and a half, and now señor Joaquín is taking her to the clinic for a check-up. That is why they have closed their establishment to the public, something that leads señor Joaquín to furrow his brow. I offer to look after the bar until they return. Señora Mercedes and señor Joaquín will not hear of it. They don't want to put me out. I convince them they are not putting me out, quite the reverse in fact.

07.12 After a rapid course of instruction into how all the most-used apparatuses in the bar function, señora Mercedes and señor Joaquín climb aboard a Seat Ibiza and depart.

07.19 Make a tour of the installations, checking all the apparatuses. Think I will be able to make them all work, apart from a very complicated one known as a tap.

07.21 Heat the coffee maker so that the clients will not have to wait for the water to heat up.

07.40 Start preparing rolls for the same reason, but as soon as I make one, I guzzle it down.

07.56 Discover a cockroach on the counter. Try to squash it with a slice of York ham, but it runs off and hides in a gap between the counter and draining board. Sits there mocking me with its antennae. You're for it. Massive dose of Baygon.

08.05 Cannot find the beer glasses anywhere. Drink with my lips against the pump. Froth comes pouring everywhere out of me. I look like a woolly sheep.

08.20 First client comes in. Pray to God he asks for something easy.

08.21 First client comes over and says good morning. I reply in like manner. Give mental instructions to the coffee machine, the fridge and the croissants to say good morning too. First client appears pleasantly surprised at this warm reception.

08.24 First client orders a coffee with milk. Horrified, I realize that the coffee machine has not heated up at all. Perhaps there's a defect, or perhaps I forgot to switch on something. Faced with the prospect of the first client leaving without having his order filled, decide to put the coffee machine lead into my nostrils and use part of my energy charge to heat it. The coffee machine blows up, but the coffee is delicious.

08.35 Just as I am trying to unstick a twenty-two egg omelette from the ceiling, señor Joaquín reappears. Before he can spot any of the damage, assure him that I will pay to replace the coffee machine, the fridge, the dishwasher, the TV, the lights and the chairs. To cheer him up, tell him there have been lots of customers. The till, which he had left empty, now contains the sum of 8 pesetas. Perhaps I did not get the change entirely right. Despite my fears, señor Joaquín does not react, as if he is not really interested in anything I have to say. He does not even seem surprised to find me up at the ceiling without a ladder. I realize that he has come back to the bar on his own, that is, without señora Mercedes. I ask what has happened.

11.35 Señor Joaquín furrows his brow and tells me they have kept señora Mercedes in hospital and are going to operate on her tomorrow. Apparently some complications have arisen which require immediate attention. As he is telling me this, we shut the bar together.

11.55 Return to the city by metro. Although all the young women travelling on the metro are gorgeous, I don't even notice them: my heart belongs to someone.

12.20 Until it is time for lunch, I inspect some of the work going on in several city centre sites. It seems to be the fashion to build more downwards than upwards. Buildings five or six storeys high have ten or fifteen underground levels, almost all of them given over to car parks or valet services. Of the two, the latter, known as valeting, is by far the more expensive. Many well-off families are faced with a terrible dilemma: should they send their children to study in the United States, or should they have a valet service for their car? Many years ago, when there were no cars, this difficulty did not exist – still less when cars and the United States did not exist. In those days of yore, buildings only had at most one underground level, called a basement and used as a wine cellar, larder or dungeon.

Yet things were not always like that either. In a very distant time, of which no traces remain in the Earth's archives, all houses were underground. The primitive men who built them imitated animal builders such as moles, rabbits, badgers and ducks (of those days), and since none of the aforementioned animals knew how to put one brick on top of another, mankind, with no other master than Nature itself, did not think of it either. In those times there were entire cities that did not show as much as an inch above ground. The houses, streets, squares, theatres and temples were all underneath. The arch-famous Babylon (not the one that appears in chronicles and history books, but another, earlier one, situated near where modern-day Zurich is to be found) was completely subterranean. It included its celebrated hanging gardens, conceived and created by an architect and gardener by the name of Abundio Greenthumb (later deified), who succeeded in growing trees and plants in a downwards direction.

14.00 Reach the spot occupied yesterday by the churro shop, only to find it is no longer there. Consternation. By asking here and there discover what has happened to it. It turns out the shop is in fact a converted van. One of its side walls can be lowered on hinges and turns into a counter. Behind this, inside the van, is where the churros are made. This system allows its owner (with proper permission from City Hall) to install the churro shop wherever the possibilities of sales are most promising. So, on weekdays, early in the mornings, it can be found up on the hill of Bonanova, where there are many schools and there is a regular clientele among the children, their companions and the teaching staff; at other times of the day it is set up in other places, for example outside the gates of Modelo Prison, where the churros are bought by lawyers visiting their clients, relatives of those clients, the prison officers guarding those clients, and even some of the clients who have succeeded in escaping;

or outside the entrance to the General Hospital's Accident and Emergency Department (cleaning staff, walking wounded and those with minor ailments who want to contract major ailments); or outside the Monumental Bullring (tourists or mad toreadors); or outside the Palace of Catalan Music (members of the Barcelona City Orchestra, wind section), and so on and so forth.

15.00 Return home. On the lift door is a sign: NOT WORKING. As this most probably refers to the lift, decide to walk upstairs.

15.02 As I pass by my neighbour's front door I come to a halt. I can hear voices from inside. I unscrew the bell, put the electric wires in my ears, and listen in. It's her! Apparently her son is reluctant to eat a plate of greens. She is trying to persuade him to eat by saying that if he doesn't, he won't grow up as big and strong as Superman; just in case that argument is not enough to persuade him, she says that if he hasn't eaten all his cauliflower in five minutes' time, she'll smash the kitchen stool over his head. I am ashamed at myself for butting into a private conversation like this, so I leave the wires dangling from the bell and carry on up the stairs.

15.15 Eat the 10 kilos of churros I have bought. Enjoy them so much that when I've finished them all I proceed to eat the greasy paper they were wrapped in.

16.00 Lying on my bed staring up at the ceiling, from which several spiders the sizes of melons are hanging. Think about my neighbour. However much I rack my brains (which I don't have), I cannot think of the best way to approach her. Knocking on her door and inviting her to dinner does not seem to me either wise or convenient. Perhaps I should offer her a gift first. On no account should I offer her money, but if I should decided to send her some, this would be better in notes than in coins. Jewels presume a more formal relationship. A perfume is a very thoughtful, but also personal gift; there is a risk that the person whom the gift is for might not like the one chosen. Laxatives, emulsions, dressings, worm powders, anti-rheumatism pills and other pharmaceutical products are definitely out. It is highly likely the woman of your dreams will adore flowers and pets. I could send her a rose and two dozen Dobermans.

17.20 Terrified by the idea that my neighbour might interpret any gift from me as disrespectful. Try to kill the spiders with Baygon.

17.45 I need clothes. Go out. Buy a pair of Bermudas. They would make me look really cool were it not for the fact that my terry cloth underpants stick out from underneath. The fact is, though, that I can't do without them because, although the climate is almost summer-like (and with a tendency to a slight rise in temperature), my metabolism has difficulty in adapting to the human body. My feet are always frozen, and so are my calves and thighs. My knees, on the other hand, are boiling; the same is true of my glutei (on one side, not the other), and so on throughout my body. The worst is my head, perhaps due to the intense intellectual activity constantly going on there. Its temperature is sometimes in excess of 150° C. In order to lessen the effects of this heat, I always wear a top hat, and fill the inside with ice cubes I buy in service stations. Unfortunately, this is only a temporary solution. The ice soon melts, the water boils and the hat is sent up into the air with such force that the first ones I had are still somewhere in the air (I have now improved the system by fastening the brim of the top hat to the collar of my shirt with a strong piece of elastic). Also bought three short-sleeved shirts (cobalt blue, yellow, maroon) a pair of deerskin moccasins I can wear without socks, and a pair of flowery swimming trunks that the young lady said would make me the hit of all the swimming pools. May God hear her.

19.00 Back in my apartment, sit watching TV and thinking. I hatch a plan to get into contact with my neighbour without raising her suspicions about my intentions. Practise in front of the mirror.

20.30 Go down to my neighbour's apartment. Knock quietly on her door. She opens it in person. Say I'm sorry to bother her at this time of night and that (though it's a lie) halfway through cooking a meal, I've realized I haven't got so much as a grain of rice. Would she be so kind as to lend me a cup of rice, which I will return to her without fail tomorrow morning, as soon as the Mercabarna opens (at five in the morning)? Think nothing of it. She gives me the cup of rice and says not to bother returning it tomorrow or any other day. That is what neighbours are there for. I thank her. We say goodbye. She shuts her front door. Run upstairs to my place and throw the rice in the bin. My plan is working even better than I could have imagined.

20.35 Knock on my neighbour's door again. She opens it herself. I ask for two spoons of rice.

20.39 Knock on my neighbour's door once more. Ask her for a clove of garlic.

20.42 Knock on my neighbour's door again. She opens it. Ask her for four peeled tomatoes, without the pips.

20.44 Knock on my neighbour's door again. She opens it. Ask for salt, pepper, parsley and saffron.

20.46 Knock on my neighbour's door again. She opens it. Ask for 200 grams of artichokes (boiled), broad beans and green beans.

20.47 Knock on my neighbour's door again. She opens it. Ask her for 1/2 kilo of peeled prawns, 100 grams of skate and 200 grams of fresh clams. She gives me 2,000 pesetas and tells me to go and eat in a restaurant and leave her in peace.

21.00 So depressed I don't even feel like eating the 12 kilos of churros I got them to send me. Eno fruit salts, pyjamas, teeth. Before going to bed, sing the responses in best baritone. Still no word from Gurb.

Day 19

07.00 It is exactly a week (in the decimal system) since Gurb disappeared, and this anniversary, together with all the reversals of fortune I have met with recently, has plunged me into despair. To ward off depression, I eat the churros left over from last night and leave home without brushing my teeth.

08.00 Appear at the cathedral, intending to light a candle to Santa Rita for Gurb's safe return. As I approach the altar, I stumble, and the candle sets light to the altar cloth. The fire is easily extinguished, but not before two geese in the cloister have been roasted. Evil omen.

08.40 Leave cathedral and go into a bar for breakfast (the earlier churros don't count). Have tuna omelette, two fried eggs with black pudding, bacon and winkles. To drink, beer (a gallon). This snack should lift my spirits, but on the contrary, the food only serves to remind me of señora Mercedes, who at this very moment must be on the operating table. Make a vow to walk up to Montserrat monastery (without dematerializing) if she comes out of this successfully.

09.00 Stroll down the Ramblas, and venture into some of the side streets. This part of the city is full of the most varied specimens of the human race, and just seeing them would be enough to confirm that Barcelona is a seaport, even if it weren't. Races from all over the world (and indeed from other worlds, if I include myself in the census) meet here, and the most contrasting destinies cross and uncross. The dregs of history have collected in this neighbourhood, which now nurtures its young: one of which, may it be said in passing, has just snitched my bag.

09.50 Continue with my stroll and the thoughts this brings to mind. In order to blend in with my surroundings, decide to adopt the appearance of a black man (but with the size and shape of Luciano Pavarotti). Of all human beings, the so-called blacks (so called because they are black) seem to be the best endowed: taller, stronger and more agile than the whites, and just as stupid. And yet the whites do not have a high opinion of them, possibly because in the collective unconscious there still exists the memory of a far-off time when the blacks were the dominant race, and the whites their slaves. The black empire's wealth came from the cultivation of fruit trees, the crops of which were almost entirely exported to the rest of the world. Since the other races spent their time hunting, as they had not yet discovered agriculture or even fishing, their diets were very harmful and they desperately needed fruit to lower their cholesterol levels. The power and opulence of the black empire lasted as long as it cultivated oranges and pears, peaches and apricots. Its decline began under Emperor Balthasar II, the great-grandfather of that other Balthasar who travelled to Bethlehem with Melchor and Gaspar. Balthasar II, nicknamed the Halfwit, had all the fruit trees of the empire pulled up, and the fertile land given over to the production of myrrh, a commodity that, then as now, had little market value.

11.00 Come to a square formed by the demolition of several blocks of buildings. In the centre there is a stiff, hairy palm tree like a porcupine. Lots of old folk drying in the sun, waiting for their relatives to come and fetch them. The poor things do not realize that many of them will never be collected, because their loved ones have gone off on cruises to the Norwegian fjords. On some benches you can see the remains of the old folk left there last summer, in a state of advanced mummification, as well as old folk who have only been there a fortnight, and are adapting to their surroundings in a less attractive way. Sit beside one of the latter, and read the literary supplement of a Madrid newspaper, which someone has abandoned on the bench for similar reasons.

12.00 Square is invaded by flocks of children who have recently escaped from their schools. They bowl hoops, and play diabolo and hide-and-seek. Seeing them only makes me feel even sadder. On my planet there is no such thing as what here is known as childhood. When we are born, the necessary (and authorized) amount of knowledge, intelligence and experience is injected into our cogitative organs. By paying a supplement you can also get an encyclopaedia, an atlas, a perpetual calendar, an endless supply of Delia Smith recipes, and the red and green versions of the Michelin guide to our beloved planet. On reaching adulthood, following an exam we are injected with the Highway Code, the municipal by-laws and a selection of the most outstanding rulings of the Court of Constitutional Affairs. But childhood – real childhood – is something we do not have. On my planet, everyone lives the life they have to lead (and nothing more) without looking for complications or getting in anyone else's way. Human beings, however, like insects, go through three phases or stages of development, if they have the time. Those in the first stage are called children; those in the second, drones; those in the third, pensioners. Children do whatever they please; so do the workers, but they get paid for it. Pensioners also receive payments, but they are not allowed to do anything, because their hands tremble and they have a habit of dropping things, apart from their sticks and the newspaper. Children have very few uses. In olden times they were used to dig coal out of mines, but progress has put a stop to this function. Now they appear on television in the afternoon, leaping about, swearing and talking an incomprehensible slang. Among human beings, as amongst us, there is a fourth (unpaid) stage, that of a stiff, upon which it is better not to dwell.

14.00 Studying the children and the old folk, and reflecting about my own existence, has saddened me still further. I shed copious tears. Since as I have already said, my human appearance is prêt-à-porter, I do not have the glands to replace what I use or expel, so that as a result of all these tears, sweat and a little goat's turd I let out a while ago, my circumstances are greatly reduced. I am now only about 40 centimetres tall. I jump off the bench and run between the legs of passers-by until I find a quiet, safe doorway where I can recover.

14.30 Decide to adopt the appearance of Manuel Vázquez Montalbán and head for his favourite restaurant, Casa Leopoldo

16.30 Return home. Call to señora Mercedes and señor Joaquín's bar to ask señor Joaquín how señora

Mercedes's operation went. A man answers who says he is a friend of señor Joaquín and is replacing him in the bar while señor Joaquín is fulfilling the (unpaid) role of accompanying señora Mercedes in the hospital, where she was operated on this morning. Thank him for the information and hang up.

16.33 Call the bar again and ask the man fulfilling señor Joaquín's role (in the bar) if the operation was a success. Yes. The operation was a success, and the result was declared satisfactory by the medical team. Thank him for the information and hang up.

16.36 Call the bar again and ask the man fulfilling señor Joaquín's role (in the bar) if señora Mercedes is allowed visitors in the hospital where she is convalescing. Yes. From tomorrow, between ten and one and four to eight. Thank him for the information and hang up.

16.39 Call the bar again and ask the man fulfilling señor Joaquín's role (in the bar) which hospital señora Mercedes is in. In Santa Tecla Hospital, in the neighbourhood of Horta. Thank him for the information and hang up.

16.42 Call the bar again and ask the man fulfilling señor Joaquín's role (in the bar) if it is possible to go by bike to Santa Tecla Hospital. He hangs up before he can give me the information or I can thank him for it. Temperature, 26° C; humidity, 74 per cent; light breezes; seas, calm.

17.00 Lie down for a siesta on the sofa, but it's so hot all my clothes stick to me. This is made worse because the sofa is covered in plastic and the cushions are filled with plastic as well, as are the springs, the legs and all the rest of the furniture in my apartment. The alternatives, that is, having things made of vegetable matter like wood or cotton, or even animal, like wool or leather, make me feel so sick that just thinking of them makes me retch. I stuff a shoe in my throat to avoid bringing up the delicious (and already paid for) grub.

17.10 Unable to sleep due to heat, so decide to adopt appearance of Mahatma Gandhi, which means I have comfortable, cool clothing and in addition an umbrella, which always comes in handy at this time of year.

17.50 Fitful sleep. Wake in turmoil, bathed in sweat. Feel an urgent need to eat churros, or failing that, to see my neighbour.

18.00 Stealthily open my apartment door. Scan the staircase. Nobody about. Go out onto landing. Stealthily close my door.

18.01 Stealthily climb the staircase. Nobody has seen me. Come to a halt stealthily outside my neighbour's door.

18.02 Stealthily apply both ears to the door of my neighbour's apartment. Hear nothing.

18.03 Stealthily examine the lock on the door of my neighbour's apartment. Fortunately, it is a maximum-security lock (the normal ones are impossible to fathom) so I can extract it without difficulty. The door opens stealthily. My heart is pounding!

18.04 Stealthily enter my neighbour's apartment. Shut the door behind me and replace the lock. The hall is simply but tastefully decorated. Leave the umbrella in the stand.

18.05 Stealthily move on to the next room which, I deduce, acts as a living room. It may well *be* a living room. Although the apartment is exactly the same as mine, the layout of the rooms is completely different, as dictated by my habits and needs. Better not go into details here.

18.07 Stealthily examine the lounge. Furnished with exquisite taste. Sit on the sofa, and cross my legs: it is both elegant and comfortable. Sit on a leather armchair and cross my legs: it is both elegant and comfortable.

Sit on an armchair with woollen upholstery. Before I can cross my legs, the armchair bites my ankle. My mistake: it wasn't an armchair, it was a mastiff, sleeping curled up in a ball.

18.09 Visit the rest of the apartment at great speed, pursued by mastiff. Decide to abandon all stealth.

18.14 Manage to escape mastiff's jaws by climbing to ceiling. The mastiff stands beneath me, waiting for me to fall. It barks horribly, and when it does so shows a set of teeth as big as bananas. As an armchair it was scary enough, but as a mastiff, it frightens the life out of me!

19.15 Been on the ceiling for an hour now, and the mastiff looks neither tired nor bored. Try hypnotizing it, but its brain is so elementary that there is hardly any difference between it being awake or asleep. Only succeed with great difficulty in making it squint, which means it no longer looks so menacing, but twice as ugly.

20.15 Two hours on the ceiling and this sonofabitch is still growling at me. In the end it is bound to get bored and go off to sleep somewhere, but I am worried at the idea that my neighbour might come back before this and find a Hindu stuck to her ceiling.

20.30 A physiological analysis of the dog shows that it has a very simple molecular structure. Perhaps therein lies the solution to my problem.

20.32 Got it! Thanks to a short, simple manipulation I have changed the mastiff into four Pekinese, and still have enough left over for a hamster. Come down from the ceiling and kick the Pekinese out of my way.

20.40 Have to hurry if I want to inspect the apartment before my neighbour returns. Or her son: strange that he is not yet back from school. Perhaps he's been punished for being an idiot.

21.00 Finish my inspection. Information I have been able to glean about my neighbour: name, Antonio Fernández Calvo; age, 56; sex, male; marital status, widower; profession, insurance salesman.

21.05 Deduce I have come to the wrong floor. Leave stealthily, put the lock back and return stealthily to my own apartment.

21.30 More down than ever. Not even the prospect of the churros the caretaker lady has brought me can cheer me up. Decide to play a game of chess against myself. Only move I can think of: PQ4. I have never really been a fan of this kind of game. Gurb was the expert. Sometimes we used to play innumerable games of chess, which he always won by fool's mate. Yield to nostalgia while eating handfuls of churros.

22.00 Put on my pyjamas. Must wash them one of these days. Get into bed and read *Delightfully Daft*, a satirical comedy in three acts. A woman will always get her way if she knows how to apply make-up where it counts. Possibly misunderstood the plot: am a little distracted by all the day's emotions. Say my prayers and go to sleep. Still no word from Gurb.

01.30 Woken by a thunderous crash. Millions (or more) years ago, the Earth was created out of a series of terrible cataclysms: the roaring oceans covered the coastline and buried whole islands, whilst gigantic mountain ranges collapsed and erupting volcanoes threw up new ones; earthquakes shifted entire continents. To commemorate these events, every night City Hall sends machines, called refuse trucks, to reproduce that planetary chaos under its inhabitants' windows. Get up, have a pee, drink a glass of water and go back to sleep.

Day 20

07.00 Weigh myself on the bathroom scales. 3.8 kilos. Given that I am pure intellect, this is dreadful. Decide to do exercise every morning.

07.30 Go out into the street, ready to run 6 miles. Tomorrow, 7; the day after, 8, and so on.

07.32 Pass a baker's. Buy a pine-nut cake and eat it on the way home. Someone else can do the running.

07.35 Going into my building, find the caretaker sweeping the doorway. Strike up a conversation that is apparently trivial but has (on my part) ulterior motives. We talk about the weather. We agree it's rather hot.

07.40 We talk about how bad the traffic is. We complain about how noisy motorbikes are.

07.50 We talk about how expensive everything is. We compare prices today to those in days gone by.

08.10 We talk about young people today. We condemn their lack of enthusiasm for everything.

08.25 We talk about the drug problem. We call for the death penalty both for those who sell it and those who buy it.

08.50 We talk about the people in the apartment block (hot! hot!).

09.00 We talk about Leibniz and the new system of nature and communication between substances (cold! cold!).

09.30 We talk about my neighbour (about time too, dammit!). The caretaker says that she (my neighbour) is a good sort and is scrupulous about paying her quarterly fees for the residents' association, but that she (my neighbour) does not attend the residents' association meetings as often as she should. I ask if she (my neighbour) is married, and she (the caretaker) replies that she (my neighbour) isn't. I ask whether I should conclude from this that she (my neighbour) had her son out of wedlock. No: she (my neighbour) was married to a pretty useless chap, according to her (the caretaker), who she (my neighbour) separated from a couple of years ago. He (the chap) takes the boy (my neighbour's and the chap's) at weekends. The judge ruled that he (the chap) had to pay her (my neighbour) alimony each month, but she (the caretaker) thinks he (the chap) does not do so as regularly as he (the chap) should. She (the caretaker) doesn't think that she (my neighbour) has any boyfriends or even casual flings. She (my neighbour) must have been warned off by her (my neighbour's) experience, she (the caretaker) thinks. But, in fact, she (the caretaker) couldn't care less about this, she (the caretaker) says. As far as she (the caretaker) is concerned, everyone should live their own life, so long as they don't create any scandal. In their own home (my neighbour's home), that is. And without making too much noise. And no later than eleven at night, which is when she (the caretaker) goes to bed. I take the broom from her (the caretaker) and smash it over her head.

10.30 Go up to my apartment. Decide to take on the appearance of D'Alembert and visit señora Mercedes in the hospital where she, God willing, is recovering from her operation.

10.50 Appear at the hospital. It is an ugly, very unwelcoming building. However, crowds of people come to it, and some even seem in a hurry to get there.

10.52 Ask at the information counter in the lobby which room I can find señora Mercedes and her companion, señor Joaquín, in. Both are in Room 602.

10.55 Walk all round the sixth floor looking for Room 602.

10.59 Find Room 602, knock on the door and señor Joaquín's voice tells me to come in. I do so.

11.00 Señora Mercedes is lying down, but is awake and looks well. I ask after her health, and she tells me that she feels weak, but is in good spirits. She has had a cup of chamomile tea this morning, she informs me. I give her the present I brought her: an electric train set. Tell her that if she is still alive tomorrow I'll bring her the siding and level crossing.

11.07 Señor Joaquín, who has had a bad night, is somewhat gloomy. He says that both he and his wife, señora Mercedes, are reaching an age when they should be taking things easy. The scare señora Mercedes has had is a warning to them, he says. He has been thinking about it all night, he says, and wonders whether they shouldn't spend the years they have left resting, travelling and allowing themselves a few treats. He is also wondering, he says, whether it is not time to pass on the bar. It's a profitable business, but it gives them a lot of headaches and it needs a young person to run it (the business) he says. He is also wondering, he says, whether I would be interested in taking it on. Señor Joaquín thinks he has spotted that I have a gift for bar management and seem to like the work.

11.10 Despite feeling weak, señora Mercedes says that she completely agrees with what her husband has just said. Both of them would like to know what I think about it.

11.12 My initial reaction is favourable. I consider myself capable of managing a bar, and think I could bring some fresh, even daring ideas to the business. For example, I think the establishment could be extended by buying the property next door (the Volkswagen car factory) and setting up a churro shop there. Señor Joaquín interrupts and says there's no hurry. In fact, he says, it was only an idea. We need to let it mature, he says. For now, he adds, it would be best for me to leave, because señora Mercedes's operation has been tough for her (señora Mercedes). She needs to rest. I leave, not before I have promised to return tomorrow to talk more about the idea.

11.30 Walk round the hospital lost in thought – and also lost. Señor Joaquín's idea has left me dazed and confused. Now that my initial enthusiasm has worn off, and looking at things more calmly, I see my first reaction was far too optimistic. It is obvious there is

Day 21

09.20 Wake filled with a strange apprehension. Takes me a while to remember what happened last night. Recalling the events helps explain my headache and why I'm feeling so sick, but not why I feel so worried. However hard I try, cannot remember when I brought the bed out onto the balcony. Nor can I remember having bought these sheets with the sexy designs on them. Shoo off the pigeons clustering on the bed-spread and get up.

09.30 There are no fruit salts in the medicine cabinet; instead, there's a bottle of peppermint. Am I losing my marbles? If so, I deserve it for being such a wretch.

09.40 Doorbell rings. When I open the door, a young man is standing there with a parcel. In the parcel are twelve linen Toni Miró suits which, according to the delivery note, I had had made yesterday. I have no idea what the boy is talking about, but don't have the strength to argue. Pay, and he leaves.

09.50 Doorbell rings. When I open the door, a young man is standing there with a box. In the box are 5 kilos of beluga caviar and a dozen bottles of Krug champagne that, according to the delivery note, I myself bought in Semon's yesterday. No idea. Pay, and he leaves.

10.00 Doorbell rings. When I open the door, there are several workmen there who say they have come to install the jacuzzi I ordered yesterday. I leave them tearing down the walls, sledgehammer in hand.

10.05 Leave the apartment somewhat confused. Descend the stairs somewhat unsteadily. To avoid an accident, decide to slide down sitting on my backside, step by step. When I go past my neighbour's door, speed up in order not to be seen in this humiliating position.

10.12 At the front door am intercepted by the caretaker, with furrowed brow. Try to avoid her, but she prevents me doing so. She says *this* cannot go on; she is very liberal minded, but she has the reputation of the building to think of, and cannot tolerate this kind of scandal here. If I want to ruin my health, throw away all my money and drag my name through the mud, that's my business, but the rest affects everyone in the building, and she will not permit it. She immediately smashes her (new) broom over my head.

10.23 Get on bus. The driver orders me off. As long as he is the driver, he says, he will not allow degenerates like me on board.

11.36 After a considerable walk, arrive at the hospital where señora Mercedes is still being kept. Before I can go in, nurses with hosepipes fumigate me from head to toe. Wonder what on earth is going on.

11.40 In Room 602 find señora Mercedes looking much better than yesterday. Señor Joaquín also seems much more optimistic. As soon as he sees me, however, he furrows his brow. He tells me that, whatever happens, I can count on him; that both he and his wife, señora Mercedes, are genuinely fond of me, and that they are both convinced that deep down I am a good person, even if I occasionally do some crazy things. After all, he says, who doesn't have something they feel ashamed of? As I have no idea what to reply, I give him the present I have brought for señora Mercedes (an Oliver Hardy death mask) and head for the door intending to leave. Before I can do so, señora Mercedes calls me back. I go over and kneel at the foot of the bed, and she kisses me on the forehead. Fat tears run down her pallid, wrinkled cheeks. We look like something from Picasso's Blue Period.

11.59 Out in the street again. Some kids throw hippopotamus dung at me. They have been to Barcelona Zoo especially to get it. And I still haven't had breakfast.

12.30 Since no taxi will stop for me however much I wave my arms about, I arrive home exhausted from walking all the way back. Without doubt I am a degenerate but I still have no idea what I have done to merit this wholesale rejection. The churro-maker refused to serve me, and even the pigeons would not greet me.

12.35 Return to my apartment. The workmen have gone, but they have installed the jacuzzi, a sauna, a dance floor, a heated swimming pool, two American bars, a nautilus, a gaming room and an opium den. All this in an apartment of 60 square metres!

12.45 Sit on the trampoline to consider what's going on. Either there is a plot against me involving all the inhabitants of this distinguished city, or I am behaving in a reprehensible manner without realizing it. Since the former is unthinkable, I have to consider the second option to be true. If this is the case, and seeing that I have always behaved in an upright fashion, it must be that there is some sort of noxious vapour on Earth that affects me. Or in Barcelona at least. Possibly I should move to Huesca, to see how I would behave there. It could also be that my circuits are going rusty.

13.30 A rustling sound rouses me from my reverie. Somebody has slipped an envelope under my door. Inside there is a single sheet of paper, on which is written the following:

> Hi there, macho. Looking for a good time?
> If you've got the money, we can help you spend it.
> Complete luxury and discretion.
> Classy atmosphere. Video sale and rental.
> Pedralbes Highway, no number (five minutes from Up & Down).

13.45 Read the message over and over. Don't know who has sent it to me, but am convinced it contains the key to the mystery. Also have no hesitation about what I must do.

14.05 Begin the physical and spiritual preparation every space warrior has to practise before combat. The Tiger position: arch my back, bend my knees, stick out my chest, fold my arms. Muscles of steel!

14.06 Cramp.

14.24 Rub Sloan liniment all over me, and continue physical and spiritual preparation every space warrior has to practise before combat. Warm up the churros left from the day before yesterday and eat them staring at myself in the mirror.

16.30 In order to penetrate the zones my steps (and my indomitable will) are leading me towards, I decide to take on the appearance of Gilbert Bécaud disguised as a Ninja turtle. Appear in the street, causing a mixture of admiration and panic.

17.00 For learning purposes, go into a multiplex to see Arnold Schwarzenegger's latest film. Agreeably surprised to find that the Government of Catalonia has financed it and that all the action takes place in Sant Llorenc, de Morunys. Cannot exclude the possibility that I am in the wrong cinema.

19.00 Leave the cinema. Go into a car salesroom. Explain to the salesman who comes over what it is I require – namely, a white Aston Martin with a special mechanism that shoots metal tacks out of the back to prevent any pursuers (of the car) catching up with it (the car). The salesman informs me that the model I want is on order but hasn't arrived yet. For the same price he sells me a Seat 850 van, which also spits out nuts and bolts through its exhaust pipe.

20.04 In calle Tuset meet the Eucharist. Accompany it three blocks intoning the *Pange Lingua*.

21.00 Ready to go into action. Sit in the driving seat. Safety belt. Helmet. Dark Jean-Pierre Gaultier glasses. Gianfranco Ferré scarf. Prince cassette. Marlboro stickers. And … vroom! Vroom!

21.05 The Diagonal is shut because of roadworks. Turn into Esplugas instead.

21.10 Esplugas also blocked by roadworks. Turn in direction of Molins del Rey.

21.20 Access to Molins del Rey blocked by roadworks. Turn onto Tarragona motorway.

22.20 Visit the Bará Arch, the Tower of the Scipios, the Archaeological Museum and the cathedral (beautiful altarpiece by Lluís Borrassà).

23.00 Start the return journey via Teruel and Soria.

01.40 Pull up outside a discreet metal gate guarded by two private security men, two policemen, two Catalan specials, two SWAT men, two men from UNCLE and a platoon from the Brunete armoured division. Obviously this place is exclusive (and excluding).

01.41 Toss the car keys in the air; the parking valet catches them.

01.42 The doorman signals me to show him my papers. Get out my ID card, my driving licence, my Catalonia Library card, the calle Vergara video club card, and the Daughters of Mary membership card. None of them is of any use.

01.43 The valet hands me back my car keys and apologizes, saying the car park is designed for BMWs, and if he parks mine he's worried he'll bump the pavement with my headlights.

01.44 In view of all the obstacles in my way, decide to abandon my attempt. Get into car and beat my retreat.

01.46 Am assailed by the memory of James Bond who, the more he was being beaten over the head, the more he persisted. As did Jerry in *Tom and Jerry*. Am ashamed of my own softness. Brake as hard as I can. Lose the crankcase, the crankshaft, the chassis and a funny sign that said:

I ♥ MY MOTHER-IN-LAW.

01.50 Return to the building lost in shadow, carrying a Swiss army knife between my teeth. Am so scary I frighten myself.

01.55 Have no problem locating the grating that covers the air conditioning. Open it with my knife, which has a screwdriver, a tin opener, a corkscrew, a saw and half-a-dozen hair-curlers (who would have thought it, seeing how serious looking the Swiss are).

02.00 Slip into the air-conditioning vent. What an adventure!

02.20 Been crawling round these disgusting metal ducts for twenty minutes now, unable to find the way out. If only I could find the hole where I came in, I'd drive home and James Bond can go boil his head.

03.00 Still crawling through the tubes. Must have covered several kilometres by now. Intense cold, because real executives are always very hot and demand air conditioning at full blast wherever they are, and all year round. It is also completely dark, but that is less important as I can see in the dark (which means I save quite a lot on electricity bills each month). This ability also enables me to steer round the obstacles I come across: rats, industrial waste, rocks and dead bodies. The dead bodies show clear signs of having frozen to death. On rapid investigation, conclude that the bodies are those of less senior executives who like me were refused entrance to the nightclub and tried to gain access in the same way as I now am.

03.40 Spot a glimmer of light in the distance. The exit! One last effort, and I'm there! A grating is blocking my way. I kick it in, then slide down the opening. Fall onto a dinner table set for twenty guests. Fortunately, none of them is there.

03.41 Hearing the crash, a waiter comes in and tells me to get off the table at once. He says this table has been reserved by Princess Stephanie of Monaco, her fiancé and her guests. In fact, he adds, the booking was made on 9 April 1978, but no one has yet appeared. Considering the class of person involved, however, the management thinks it best not to cancel the booking. Once a week, the waiter goes on, the tablecloths and napkins are laundered, the cutlery is polished, the floral decorations are renewed, the ants are exterminated and the rolls (white, wholemeal and soya bread) are replaced by freshly baked ones. In a corner are half-a-dozen photographers covered in cobwebs.

03.44 Recovered from my fall, and the waiter says I am welcome to dine at any of the other free tables. This in fact means all of them, because truly elegant people never dine before five or half-past five in the morning, so as not to be taken for the hoi polloi who have to get up early. Reply that for the moment I'd like a glass of champagne at the bar.

03.45 As champagne does not agree with me, pass the time counting the bubbles that the liquid inexplicably produces, and listening to the conversation of three men who are at the bar with me. Their conversation might be interesting but for the fact that they have drunk so much champagne they burp all the time and are incomprehensible. Yet it is not difficult to guess what they are talking about, because Catalans always talk about the same thing, namely work. As soon as two or more Catalans are gathered together, each of them talks about his job in great detail. Using only seven or eight terms (sole rights, commissions, order book and a few more) they construct the liveliest of debates, which can go on forever. In the entire world there is nobody as dedicated to work as the Catalans. If only they knew how to do something, they would rule the Earth.

04.00 A very young and attractive woman comes up to me. Without any show of embarrassment, she asks me if I study or work. I reply that, when properly considered, the distinction is a false one, because a person who studies anything seriously is doing important work (for the future), whereas a person who works with all his five senses will of necessity be learning something new every day. Doubtless satisfied by my answer, the young woman moves swiftly away.

06.00 Time passes without me unearthing any of the clues I was looking for. I begin to think that my intuition has failed me for the first time ever. People have arrived, had dinner and are leaving. Some of them have slimmed so much during their business dinners that they have vanished before the coffee. And I'm still stuck here like a lemon watching the world go by and counting champagne bubbles. My glass has already been changed four times so I can go on amusing myself. Am on the point of leaving.

06.05 Only person left in the entire building. Feel extremely sleepy. I even think I may have nodded off without meaning to, as the bar in front of me has got several dents in it. Ask for the bill so that I can leave, and abandon my investigation.

06.16 While I am considering the least dangerous way of getting down from my bar stool, a man on his own arrives. He puts his left elbow on the bar and clicks the fingers of his right hand. The waiter comes over and the man orders a whisky. What brand? Malt. Tall glass? No. With ice? Yes. Two cubes? Three. Any water? Yes. Mineral water? Yes. Still or sparkling? Still. The waiter moves away. The man passes out.

06.20 Practise mouth-to-mouth respiration on the man and slap him on the cheeks to bring him round. As I try to do both things at the same time, find I receive most of the slaps myself.

06.25 Man regains consciousness just as the waiter brings his drink. He downs it in one. Falls flat again. I renew my efforts.

07.00 Man and I leave the place together. He leans on me, I lean on the walls. Outside, the birds are trilling on the branches and the sun's cheery countenance appears over the horizon, which indicates to me that we are already in …

Day 22

07.00 Same as the preceding paragraph.

07.05 With a strength I would never have imagined in such a pathetic creature, my new friend and dependant tears himself from my arms. In fact, he tears off my arms. While I am putting them back, he apologizes profusely. For goodness sake, it's not the slightest bit important. My new friend and dependant explains that, despite appearances, he is not drunk. Merely tired and emotional. He has had several sleepless nights. Several sleepless months. I ask the reason for this.

07.30 The travails of an executive: reading and only partially understanding prices on the stock market, currency market, futures market; semi-skimmed milk with coffee, toast with margarine, pills; shower, shave, brisk application of aftershave. The executive dons his apparel: Ermenegildo Zegna here, Ermenegildo Zegna there, Ermenegildo Zegna everywhere. The children – washed, clothed and brushed – are put into the executive's saloon. Papa is taking them to school. They had dinner last night at their mother's, but slept at their father's. Tonight they are going to eat at their father's, but sleep at their mother's; she will take them to school tomorrow, but he will go and fetch them so they can have dinner at his house or their mother's (they'll call each other). One of the children is his; the other one he has never seen in his life before, but he prefers not to ask. Ever since his separation from his wife (they're still friends) he prefers not to ask anyone anything. The executive drives the car with his knees; in his right hand he holds the car mobile phone; with his left hand he tunes in the radio; with his left elbow he raises and lowers the car windows; with his right elbow he stops the kids playing with the gear stick; he uses his chin to constantly sound the horn. At the office: telexes, faxes, letters, messages on the answering machine; he consults his diary. Kelly, cancel my meeting at eleven; Kelly, fix me a meeting at twelve; Kelly, book me a table for four at La Dorada; Kelly, cancel the table I've booked at Reno's; Kelly, book me a flight to Munich tomorrow; Kelly, cancel this afternoon's flight to Geneva; Kelly, my pills. The executive uses any brief pauses in his busy schedule to learn English:

My name is Pepe Rovelló,
In shape no bigger than an agate stone
On the forefinger of an alderman,
Drawn with a team of little atomies
Athwart men's noses as they lie asleep.

The executive dances flamenco. His teacher scolds him because it is obvious he has not been practising at home. 'C'mon, Rovelló, let's be seein' ya move that arm and waist of yours!' The executive practises the difficult art of playing castanets on his Kawasaki. As a result of the accident, he arrives late at his club. Plays two games of squash still wearing his flamenco outfit. At the restaurant all he has is a plate of celery (without salt), a mint pastille and a Cohiba cigar. Pills, digestive syrup, multivitamins. The executive's ailments: gastritis, sinusitis, migraines, circulation problems, chronic constipation. He confuses his Cohiba with a suppository. In his aerobics class he dislocates his bones; the chiropractor puts them back in place; the masseuse dislocates them again. A problem: his second ex-wife is pregnant by the ex-husband of his first ex-wife: a) what names to give the newborn baby? b) who pays for the scans? One last problem: the crew on his yacht has mutinied and taken up piracy off the Costa Dorada.

07.50 The executive and I say goodbye. He's had one for the road, he says, and can start the day with the no way I can take on the bar. The possibility of renting or buying a bar with a view to making money is not even mentioned in the orders we were given at the start of our space mission. Of course, there was no strict prohibition to doing so either. I would need to consult. Temperature, 26° C; humidity, 70 per cent; seas, slightly choppy.

12.30 Still walking round the hospital, unable to find a way out of my deliberations or the hospital. Do, however, find the canteen. Decide to have a break and get something to eat, even though it is rather early. You always think better on a full stomach, say those who have a stomach.

12.31 The canteen is empty. Fortunately, the counter is well stocked and I really like the self-service system, because it allows me to eat as much as I like without having to justify myself to anyone. If I like dipping these Padron peppers in milky coffee, whose business is it but mine, eh?

13.00 The more I eat and the more I think, the more ridiculous I find the idea of remaining on Earth. It would mean abandoning the mission that Gurb (missing) and I were entrusted with. That would be a real betrayal. That argument, however, is unconvincing because it basically comes down to a question of principle, and to me principles are what human beings call so many arse wipes. More weighty, though, is the physiological argument. I have no idea how long my organism can stand up to the living conditions on such a miserable planet as this. I have no idea what kinds of peril threaten(s) me. I do not even know if my presence here constitutes a danger to human beings or not. It is clear that my odd constitution and the energy charge I have cause problems wherever I go. It cannot be coincidence that the lift in my apartment block is always out of order, or that the TV programmes always start late when I want to watch (or record) them. Even now, while I was walking around the corridors of the hospital, I heard a conversation that alarmed me. A doctor was telling a nurse, with furrowed brow, that all the machines in the hospital seemed to have gone crazy this morning. Apparently, the patients in the intensive care unit were dancing the lambada and the scanner showed pictures of Judy Garland singing 'Somewhere Over the Rainbow'. These inexplicable events, added the doctor, once again furrowing his brow, had begun precisely at 10.50. As if at that moment, he concluded, a Martian had entered the building. I was offended that anybody could compare me to one of those snobs who spend all their time playing golf and complaining about the service, but I made sure I kept this to myself.

Of course, there was always the possibility of modifying my molecular structure to that of human beings. If I decided to do that, I would have to choose my model carefully, because the process would be irreversible. What a momentous decision! What would happen if, once I had changed, I found I wasn't happy? What would become of me if the affair with my neighbour ended up like the foggy, foggy dew? Would I be able to live with the yearning nostalgia I would feel for my native planet? What would the economic situation be like in the post-Olympic era? So many imponderables! If only I had someone to share my troubles with!

13.30 Decide to leave the canteen. When I try to pay for my food, discover this was not a self-service restaurant. In fact, the place where I have been eating was not a canteen at all. Leave without being seen.

14.15 Sit and think on a bench in the Plaza Cataluña. Without a doubt, the best thing to do would be to conclude our mission to Earth and return home. I have no idea whether the mission's objectives have been achieved, but when all's said and done, that doesn't really matter. Nobody is going to read our report anyway. The main problem comes from the fact that I cannot return on my own. The spaceship is still out of action, and I don't know how to fix it. Even if it fixed itself, I wouldn't know how to start it up, still less how to pilot it. These ships are made for a two-being crew. That is meant to prevent any sly being stealing the ship for their own purposes, like going on a date or using it as a taxi. I could ask for help from Space Station AF in the constellation of Antares, but that wouldn't be much good either. Even if they sent another ship to rescue me, that would have a two-being crew as well, and if one of them came with me, who would get the other one back?

15.00 Decide to abandon my thoughts and the Plaza Cataluña, because the pigeons have covered me in shit from head to toe, and several Japanese tourists are taking photos of me, thinking I must be a national monument.

15.45 At home. The apartment is very hot, especially at this time of day. I would put in air conditioning, but the vibrations play hell with my joints. It's the same with the fridge: it goes quiet for a while, but then suddenly without warning starts a Saint Vitus's dance that drives me crazy. And yesterday, for example, no sooner had I switched on the mixer than I broke my femur in three places. Thank heavens I have spare parts. The fan is more acceptable, except that when it is going round I get seasick, because I can't take my eyes off the blades. In the end it's better to do without all these gadgets and gradually strip off as the temperature rises. Soon I'm in a T-shirt and socks.

17.00 In all the universe, there is nothing so carelessly slung together as the human body. Just looking at the ears, stuck on to the side of the head any old how, would be enough to disqualify it. The feet are ridiculous; the intestines, revolting. And every skull is a grinning absurdity. Yet human beings are only partly to blame for all this. The fact is that they were very unlucky with evolution.

18.00 Go out for a walk. The streets are busier than usual because, now the days are hot, every self-respecting inhabitant of Barcelona wants to take his place on the terraces that bars set up on the pavements between rubbish bins. There every self-respecting inhabitant is deafened, polluted and poisoned. They then pay for the privilege and go home. Encouraged by the spectacle, I buy an ice-cream cornet. Since this is the first time I have ever consumed anything like this, I first eat the cornet. Then I have no idea what to do with the ball of ice cream; I get into a mess, lose my head and throw all that's left into a waste-paper bin.

18.40 Returning from my walk, catch sight of my neighbour in the distance. A truly providential encounter. In order not to seem bad mannered, avoid being seen, but decide I will bring our relationship out into the open this very day. At the stationer's buy writing materials; at the post office buy stamps. Temperature, 28° C; humidity, 79 per cent; no wind to speak of; seas, calm.

19.00 Lock myself in my apartment, brush my teeth and lay out on the desk everything I need to write a letter: a ream of paper, highlighter, inkwell, ruler, blotting paper, a ballpoint pen (just in case), the María Moliner dictionary, a correspondence manual (love letters and commercial), a dictionary of rhymes, the Sáinz de Robles anthology of Spanish poetry and the *El País* style guide.

19.45 'My adorable neighbour,

I am a very good-looking young man, who is both romantic and affectionate. I enjoy a good economic situation and am very serious about serious things (but I like to have fun too). Besides churros, I am crazy about travelling on the metro, shining my shoes, window shopping, seeing how far I can spit, and girls. I detest greenery in all shapes and forms, cleaning my teeth, writing postcards and listening to the radio. I think I would make a good husband (should the occasion arise) and father (I am very patient with children). Would you like to get to know me better? I'll be expecting you at 9.30. There will be food (free) and drink. We can talk about everything I've mentioned, and other things too (ho, ho). RSVP. Mad about you ...'

19.55 Read what I've written. Tear up the letter.

20.55 'My dear neighbour,

Since we live in the same building, I thought it might be a good idea to get better acquainted. Come this evening at 9.30. I'll make some supper and we can discuss matters related to the apartment block (and other things as well).

Best wishes.

Your neighbour.'

21.05 Read what I've written. Tear up the letter.

21.20 'Dear neighbour,

I've got stuff in the fridge that won't keep. Why don't you come up so we can polish it off? We could talk about the apartment block and the repairs it needs (new motor for the lift, repainting the front, and so on). I'll be expecting you at 10.

Faithfully yours,

A neighbour.'

Read what I've written. Tear up the letter.

22.00 'My apartment is full of cracks ...'

22.20 'I've got food full of worms ...'

23.00 Go out and eat alone in the Chinese restaurant on the corner. As I am the only customer, the owner of the establishment sits at my table and starts talking. His name is Jesus Mai Fut (he was baptized by a clumsy missionary), and was born in Kiang-Si. As a boy he emigrated to San Francisco, but caught the wrong boat and ended up in Barcelona. As he has never learned the Latin alphabet, he has still not realized his mistake, and I do not feel it's my job to put him right. He is married and had four children: Jesus Junior (his eldest boy), Chiang, Wong and Sergei. He works all hours of the day, from Monday to Saturday. Sunday is his day off, and he usually spends it with his entire family looking (in vain) for the Golden Gate Bridge. He tells me he hopes one day to return to China; that is why he works and saves. He asks me what I do. So as not to confuse him, I say I am a bolero singer. He says he loves boleros, because they remind him of his beloved country of Kiang-Si. He offers me a glass of Chinese brandy, which he himself makes from all the leftovers his customers leave on their plates. The brandy is a dark, thick brown colour: its taste is difficult to describe, but is very aromatic.

00.00 We sing 'Kiss Me Like You Love Me'. Another glass of brandy.

00.05 We sing 'When I'm With You'. Another glass.

00.10 We sing 'Used to You'. Another glass.

00.15 We make silly pigtails from pasta, sing 'Last Night I Talked to the Moon', and leave to look for the Golden Gate Bridge. Take the bottle along to help us on our way.

00.30 Go down calle Balmes singing 'Face to Face Again', and asking everyone if they have seen a suspension bridge. What a lark!

00.50 Sit in the entrance to the Banco Atlántico and sing 'Be Careful with Your Lies'. Cry on each other's shoulders.

01.20 Sit on the cathedral steps and sing 'Allow Me to Applaud the Way You Hurt Me'. Cry on each other's shoulders.

01.40 Lie on the ground in the plaza de San Felipe Neri. Sing 'Worse for Me Was Your Love'. Cry on each other's shoulders.

02.00 Run round the Sagrada Familia singing at the tops of our voices. Can't find the Golden Gate Bridge anywhere, but Subirachs pokes his head out of a window to see what's going on. We sing 'I'm Going to Switch Off the Light to Think of You' in his honour.

02.20 We hail a taxi, get in and tell the driver to take us to China. In the taxi we sing 'I Forgot I Had Forgotten You'.

02.30 Taxi driver dumps us outside the police station, and even charges us the fare. We do not give him a cent in tips.

02.55 Cautioned by the authorities, I return home. Crawl up the stairs. Hope to God my neighbour does not see me in this deplorable state.

03.10 The room is spinning round. Groan my prayers and crawl into bed. Still no word from Gurb.

satisfaction of someone who has done his duty. He puts on his helmet and gloves. Ask him if he is sure he is up to driving a motorbike. What! Motorbike? Who do I take him for? He always travels to the city by hang-glider.

08.00 Run up and down the Pedralbes highway, and succeed in getting him airborne. I let the line go. My friend waves goodbye from the blue of the morning sky: farewell, farewell, we'll always have Ampurdán.

08.05 Try to return home dragging my feet. Either this (colloquial) expression does not fit reality or there is a way of moving forwards dragging both feet at the same time that is beyond me. I try dragging just one foot and hopping with the other. Fall in a heap.

08.06 While reflecting on the meaning of the word 'heap', I see a wallet on the road in front of me. A rapid analysis indicates that the wallet began life belonging to a crocodile. A more detailed analysis tells me the wallet has passed through several hands and finally belonged, until it was lost, to my friend the executive. Now it belongs to whatever my peculiar sense of honesty dictates, ho, ho. Temperature, 23° C; humidity, 56 per cent; light easterly breeze; seas, choppy.

08.07 Examine the contents of the executive's wallet. Three or four thousand in notes. Slip them into my pocket immediately. ID card, driving licence, credit cards and cards showing their owner belonged to the world of thrusting leaders of men. Photo of a wolf-hound standing next to a tree. Nothing in any of it for me.

08.10 About to throw the wallet and its contents down a drain when I discover a compartment shut by a zip. Struggle with it. Unable to master this strange mechanism (or to understand how something so absurd could have become so commonplace), so in the end break it open. Take a photo from inside. An extremely good-looking young lady. On the back, a short dedication: 'Hi there, Sweetie-pie – who loves you? Your Cuqui.'

08.11 Aha!

08.12 Decide to return home. A taxi goes by – stop it, get in. On the way home, listen to the radio news. Another accident at the nearby nuclear reactor at Vandellós. A spokesman for the nuclear facility informs the public of all the advantages of life as a mutant. Surprise your family every morning! he says. The taxi driver is not convinced. If he were in charge, he says, he would transfer the reactor to the Coto de Doñana. That would teach all those blasted protected species over there, he says.

08.30 Hurry to get into my apartment. The hostility of my neighbours increases all the time. The caretaker has become a Cerberus with her broom, and shoots darts dipped in curare at me. One resident pours cauldrons of boiling oil down the stairwell each time I appear. Another has slipped tarantulas into my living room. Forced to use almost a whole can of Baygon.

08.45 Decide I have to clear up the misunderstanding. This afternoon I'll get all the residents together, offer them some tea, listen (patiently) to their complaints and try to rehabilitate myself in their eyes. If any of them would like a dip in my pool for free, they're welcome.

08.50 Go out to buy all the items for the treat I'm offering. Take on the appearance of Alfonso the Fifth (The Magnanimous, 1396–1458) and stride out.

09.00 Buy two-dozen brioches, a pat of butter, 100 grams of mortadela, a bottle of pop.

09.10 Buy little paper lanterns, balloons, streamers.

09.20 Return home. Scorpions in my letter box, cobra in the lift, napalm on the landing outside my apartment.

09.50 Finish preparing the buffet. The results are not very satisfactory, possibly because I did not have a knife and so was forced to use pliers.

10.00 Write out the invitations. 'I have the pleasure of inviting don ... and señora to a reception to be held, blah, blah ... Dark lounge suit advisable', and so on and so forth. They look lovely.

10.05 Place the invites in their respective envelopes. Lick the sticky strip on the envelopes so that they will stick (to themselves). The gum is so tasty I can't avoid eating three envelopes together with their invitations. As I am doing all this, reflect on how happy I would be if only things worked out as I would like: señora Mercedes's bar, my downstairs neighbour, etc. Count the days to Christmas.

10.15 A rustling sound rouses me from my reverie. Somebody has slipped an envelope under my door. No sign of who it is from. Inside there is a single printed sheet, which says:

> So, did you enjoy last night?
> Tonight could be even better
> If you paid me a visit. I'm a slice
> Of Heaven with syrup and honey, aromas
> And conserving agents (E413, E462)
> Just for your Tiger mouth.
> 5, Calle del Turrón de Yema, 2nd penthouse.
> (On the corner of Traversera de las Corts).
> P.S. Forget those neighbours of yours,
> They are only jealous.

10.25 Since somebody seems determined to spoil my reintegration into society, tear up the invitations, eat all the brioches and set fire to all the little lanterns. Make a Hawaiian skirt with the streamers.

10.40 Have a bit of a dance, but soon get bored.

10.45 Call the hospital where señora Mercedes is convalescing. Talk to señor Joaquín. How are things? Fine, just fine. The doctor says señora Mercedes can go home whenever she likes. And señor Joaquín as well, of course. They will possibly both be back at the bar tomorrow. That is good news, and I am very pleased. We hang up.

11.00 It is a sunny, clear, dry morning, not as hot as on recent days. Decide to go out. But where to?

11.05 Decide to visit an art gallery, something I know little about. The fact is that on my planet we don't consider the plastic arts as very important, partly because we are congenitally colour blind and myopic, and partly because we couldn't give a stuff about aesthetics. For this reason, and also due to my natural disinclination to (and lack of talent for) study, my education in this area is somewhat deficient. If someone were to ask me who the painters I know were, I would say: Piero della Francesca and Tàpies, and that's your lot.

11.30 Appear at the Museum of Catalan Art. Closed for repairs.

11.45 Appear at the Museum of Contemporary Art. Closed for repairs.

11.45 Appear at the Ethnological Museum. Closed for repairs.

12.20 Appear at the Museum of Modern Art. Closed for repairs. The female director explains that the relevant authority has decided to refurbish the museum and convert it into a multi-sectorial, inter-disciplinary centre, and if the funds permit, an interactive play centre as well. To this end they are constructing a fifteen-storey building that will house two theatres, four cafés, a souvenir shop, an old people's home, the current painting collection, the distorting mirrors from the Tibidabo amusement park and the Planelles collection of sticking plasters. The construction work, originally scheduled for completion by 1992, cannot even be started until 1998. During the changes, the works of art have been stored in the port warehouses that another municipal committee ordered knocked down last month. At this point in time, therefore, it is highly likely that all the pictures are floating somewhere in the Mediterranean. However, she adds, if I would like to visit the museum I will not be disappointed, because that very morning they have taken delivery of a woolly mammoth to be stored until the refurbishment of the Natural History Museum (currently closed for repairs) is complete.

13.00 Since I am in the Parque de la Ciudadela, decide to spend the rest of the morning here. At a kiosk I buy a family-size box of Estepa sweets. Sit to eat them next to the pond, and since the noonday sun is beating down, nobody tries to take my chair from me. Some ducks come gliding over. Feed them sweets, they eat them and sink straight to the bottom of the pond.

14.00 Lunch at the Siete Puertas. Elvers, prawns, kidneys, sweetbreads, Bath chaps stew, two bottles of Vega Sicilia, Catalan custard, coffee, brandy, Monte-cristo No. 2 and I'm past caring.

16.30 Climb up to Montjuich Castle to help digest lunch.

17.30 Walk down from Montjuich Castle to help digest lunch.

18.30 Climb back up to Montjuich Castle to help digest lunch.

19.00 Tea in the Calle Petrixol.

20.00 Head for place of rendezvous, arriving at 20.32.

20.32 See above.

20.33 As I enter the lobby of the building, am stopped by an elegantly uniformed doorman. Where do I think I am going? To the second penthouse, señor doorman. Oh, yes? And might one know why I am going to the second penthouse? To see someone I have an appointment with. Oh, an appointment, an appointment, that's easy enough to say. Let's see, sweetheart: who is this *someone* you have *an appointment* with, like? It's a young lady, but for the life of me, I can't remember her name. Oh, a young lady ... perhaps you mean señorita Piloski? Yes, absolutely, that's the one. Well, your luck's out, my lad, because señorita Piloski died forty years ago, just when I first started as doorman in this building, which I have the honour of protecting from intruders and ne'er do wells. All right, all right, perhaps that wasn't her name. Perhaps you meant señorita Sotillo, may God rest her soul.

21.30 After we have gone through fifty-two señoritas and said a prayer for the eternal peace of each of their souls, I decide to give him a 5,000-peseta note.

21.31 The doorman himself accompanies me in the lift, humming a tune to himself so as not to lose his musical thread.

21.32 The doorman leaves me alone on the landing. Ring the bell: ding-dong. Silence. Ding-dong. Nothing. Fortunately, there is a flowerpot on the landing, so I relieve myself in it. Just nerves.

21.34 Insist. Ding-dong. The rustle of steps coming towards the door. A spyhole opens. An eye observes me. If I had a toothpick with me, I'd poke it out.

21.35 Spyhole closes. The footsteps move away. Silence.

21.36 Footsteps draw closer again. Sound of a bolt being drawn back. The door swings slowly open. What about running off downstairs? No, no, I'll stay.

21.37 The door opens wide. A señora in dressing gown and slippers hands me her refuse bag, then immediately apologizes. What with the dark landing and not having her glasses on, she mistook me for the doorman. He always comes at this time of night, you know. Yes, I must have got the wrong door. The young lady I'm looking for lives opposite. No, I didn't disturb her. Yes, lots of gentlemen make the same mistake. Nerves, obviously. And yes, they all end up peeing in the yucca: that's why it's so nice and shiny. Since I'm there, would I mind putting out her rubbish? *The Simpsons* is about to start and she doesn't want to miss it. Yes, it can be rude, but at her age she's seen it all.

Anyway, you should be getting on or you'll have to take the rubbish to the container outside.

21.45 Travel back up in the lift. Ring the bell on the other door.

21.47 A man opens it. Have I got it wrong again? No, the señorita is expecting me. Please, come this way.

21.48 We go down a corridor: fitted carpet, curtains, paintings, flowers, intoxicating perfume. I'll be lucky to get out of here alive.

21.49 We come to a halt in front of a door upholstered in crimson velvet. The fellow accompanying me tells me the señorita is behind it. Waiting for me. He, if I had not already guessed it from his dress and manners, is the butler. In fact, he says, he's a black belt at karate. So no funny business, right? I promise. Still don't understand what the word 'butler' means, but his tone of voice doesn't allow for any questioning.

21.50 Door opens. Hesitate. A voice tells me to come in: come on, don't be shy. Can it be possible?

21.51 It *is* possible!

02.40 We hardly notice the time telling each other our adventures. Gurb has been unlucky too. First it was the university professor. He was attracted to him (the professor) but had to leave him because he insisted he (Gurb) should do a thesis. He was looking for a serious man with a bit of class about him, like Patrick Swayze, but without knowing why or how, it seemed he always ended up falling in love with bums. I tell him that's because he's become a tart. Gurb replies that's not true, the thing is I have always been a moaner. We get into a heated argument, until the butler steps in to remind us (as discreetly as possible) that two extraterrestrials on a special mission should not be wasting time arguing like a pair of fishwives. Especially over such trivialities. If he wanted to, he says, he could tell us some really moving stories. Stories, he says, which would move us to tears. Because he, he says, is a man who has seen a thing or two. There were fifteen in his family. In fact, he was an only child, but he had two parents, four grandparents and eight great-grandparents, none of who seemed anxious to pop their clogs. As a boy they were all so hungry that they ate their ration cards before they could exchange them for rice, lentils, black bread and powdered milk. Hearing all these misfortunes, and before his story can drag on endlessly, we shed copious tears, pay him for the days he has already worked and fire him.

02.45 Gurb shows me round his apartment. Fantastic! He tells me he chose everything himself. Compare (silently) his apartment with my own and blush with shame.

02.50 Gurb opens a heavy wooden door and shows me what he has just had installed: a sauna. Of course, he has never used it and never will, but it's a good place to keep his churros hot.

02.52 While I'm stuffing my face with churros, I ask if he is the one responsible for all my recent problems. He says he is, but with the best of intentions. One advantage of telepathic communication is that you can talk with your mouth full. Ask him why he wants to sabotage the life I was hoping to lead, turning me into debauched rake in everyone's eyes. He replies that he could not allow me to end up serving coffee in señora Mercedes and señor Joaquín's bar, still less having a romance with my neighbour, although the likelihood of that happening, he adds sarcastically, was remote, given the way I was handling things. That starts another argument, until the doorbell rings. We go to open the door. It's the next-door neighbour, complaining he can't sleep for the noise. He says that if we want to fight, we should do it out loud, like normal people, because he's used to shouting and broken plates. But our telepathic communication interferes with his TV set, and he's fed up with it.

03.00 Since it has grown so late, we decide to go to sleep and continue our conversation in the morning. Before going to bed, we say the rosary together. During the second mystery (the mystery of joy) I have to tell Gurb off, because I catch him sneaking a look at a copy of *La Maison de Marie Claire*.

03.15 Force Gurb to clean his teeth. Heaven knows how long it is since he's brushed them *comme il faut*.

03.20 Ask Gurb if he has got something I can wear in bed. He shows me his lingerie cupboard. Prefer not to look.

03.30 Gurb settles down in his bed; I'm on the sofa in the living room. We leave the door ajar. Good night, Gurb. See you in the morning. Have a good sleep. You too. Sweet dreams, Gurb.

03.50 Gurb? What is it? Are you asleep? No, what about you? Me neither. Would you like a glass of milk? No, thanks.

04.10 Gurb? What is it? What are you thinking about? Nothing, and you? I was thinking that, now we've found each other, at last we can return to our beloved planet. Ah.

04.20 Still awake? What is it, Gurb? Do you want to return to our beloved planet? Of course: don't you? Oh, I don't know what to say. The fact is, our beloved planet is a real drag. Oh, come on, Gurb, you may be right to some extent, but what choice do we have? Well, we could stay here. And do what? Oh, I don't know, heaps of things. Like what, for example? We could run a bar between us. Oh, that's rich: when I wanted to take over señora Mercedes and señor Joaquín's bar you did all you could to stop me; but now it's you who is suggesting it, all of a sudden I'm supposed to like the idea. There's no comparison; señora Mercedes and señor Joaquín's bar was full of pensioners, but what I'm proposing would be something else entirely: top design, live music, pool tables, tarot, open all night, and on Saturdays, Miss Tanga contests. Hmm. Promise me you'll think about it. I promise.

04.45 Gurb, are you there? What is it? Do you think that would make money? Bah, who thinks of money? I do. OK, don't worry, that sort of place always makes a fortune. Yes, at first they do, but then the next year somewhere else becomes hot and you can stuff your design you know where. So what? When the business starts to fade, we open another one. This city is a gold mine; and when we get tired of it, we can always go to Madrid. Sweetheart, that's paradise: just using the air shuttle makes it worthwhile. I don't know, I don't know; I'm not sure if it all adds up. Look, if you're worried about the future, all you have to do is take out a pension plan: with a life expectancy of 9,000 years, you'd drive the bank crazy. Now let me sleep, will you? OK, Gurb, don't get angry again. I'm not angry, but go to sleep. Good night, Gurb. Good night.

Day 23

10.13 Woken by the doorbell. Where am I? On a sofa. Whose is this stylish living room? Ah, now I remember. Where's Gurb? His bedroom door is shut. He must be sleeping like a log. He always was a sleepyhead. Not like me, early to bed and early to rise. The doorbell is still ringing.

10.15 Tap gently on the bedroom door. No reply. Decide to answer the front door myself.

10.16 Open the door. A young man carrying a bouquet of lilies is standing there. For the señorita, he says. I give him a couple of coins as a tip and he hands over the bouquet. Shut the door.

10.18 In the kitchen. Note down the two coins I paid from my own pocket when Gurb should have been the one to cough up. Look for a vase. When I find it, fill it with water and display the flowers as best I can. The result leaves a lot to be desired. Perhaps I shouldn't have cut the stems so much. Too late to be sorry.

10.21 Open the envelope pinned to the bouquet. Contains a hand-written card. I shouldn't read what it says, but I do. 'To my darling Cuqui with a million kisses mwa mwa mwa mwa mwa mwa mwa mwa mwa, Pepe.'

10.24 Doorbell again. Decide to answer it myself. Young man with a box of frozen truffles. Two more coins.

10.26 Note down my expenditure. Put the box of truffles in the freezer. Take it out, eat ten truffles, rearrange the others so no one will notice, then put the box back in the freezer. Read the card. Would not dare repeat what it says. Temperature, 57° C; humidity, 75 per cent; light southwesterly breezes; seas, choppy.

10.29 Doorbell rings. Decide to answer it myself. A young man carrying a basket. In the basket, a bar of perfumed soap, bath gel, moisturizing cream, body milk, sponge, eau de toilette. Two coins. Take the samples to the bathroom. Throw the card down the toilet (without reading it) and pull the chain. Note down the expenditure. Doorbell rings.

10.32 Decide to answer it myself. This time it's not a young man, but a great hairy brute. His hands are empty, and he says he wants to speak to the lady of the house. Reply that the lady of the house is not free at the moment. If he wishes, I add, he can come back later or leave me his card. The brute asks if by chance I am the lady of the house's husband. No sir, no way. Her boyfriend, then? No. Her friend? No again. So, who am I and what the hell am I doing here? I'm the butler, I reply, and I'm a karate expert; so no funny business, right?

10.34 The brute calms down and leaves. At least I didn't have to pay him anything.

10.36 As I crawl towards the kitchen feeling for the corridor walls, bump into Gurb. The noise from me hitting the mat, the doorframe and the lintel woke him up. Tell him what happened and instead of feeling sorry for me, he bursts out laughing. When he sees me furrow my brow he stifles the silly giggle he's adopted from heaven knows where and tells me the brute is a jealous suitor who has been pursuing him for days. The day before he knocked out two teeth of the previous butler with a swipe of his hand. He's very violent and passionate, says Gurb, that's why he likes him.

10.40 Use oxygenated water on my wounds. I'm so covered in bumps and bruises that I change my appearance to Tutmosis II to save the trouble of putting on all those bandages.

11.00 Leaving the bathroom, hear Gurb's voice calling from the terrace. Go out and discover (with pleasure) that he has prepared breakfast and served it on a small marble table under a parasol. Disappointment: half a grapefruit, lemon tea, toast with butter and English marmalade. I miss the aubergine omelette and beer I get at señora Mercedes and señor Joaquín's bar, but I eat what I'm given and keep shtum. Notice that the windows and flat roofs all around are bristling with binoculars, field glasses and telescopes, all of them focused on Gurb's salmon-coloured dressing gown. Consider the possibility of zapping all these peeping Toms with a death ray, but choose instead to pretend I don't see what is going on.

11.10 We polish off breakfast in no time. Gurb lights a cigarette. I pretend to have a dreadful cough to get him to understand that smoke is not only a nuisance but extremely harmful. If he wants to poison himself, that's his business, but that is no reason to force the rest of us to breathe in his polluted air. The healthy message implicit in my fit of coughing goes unnoticed: Gurb carries on smoking, and my throat becomes red raw.

11.15 Ask Gurb if he was serious about what he was saying last night. In return, Gurb asks me what in particular I am referring to. The trendy nite spot: what else? Of course he was being serious. And the Miss Tanga contests? Was he serious about that too?

Of course, he says. What about me: could I be the presenter? Naturally, he says. And put the sash on the winner? Whatever I like, he says; being the owner has to have some advantages.

11.20 Clear away the breakfast things, take them to the kitchen. Gurb stays on the terrace reading *La Vanguardia*. Put the plates, cups and cutlery in the dishwasher.

11.30 Polish the silver.

12.30 Vacuum the floors. Change the bag.

13.00 Clean the windows. Pray to God it doesn't start to rain.

13.30 Put a wash on. Iron sheets. Find an old, torn sheet, make rags out of it.

14.00 Ask Gurb what time of day lunch is served in this establishment. Reply: lunch is not served in this establishment. As far as he (Gurb, that is) is concerned, he has a rendezvous in half an hour's time in the Café de Colombia, the Vaquería and the Dorado Petit (the one in Barcelona and the one in Sant Feliu). He always accepts three invitations at a time, he says, and then makes up his mind at the last moment which one to go to. As for me, I can rustle up something from whatever is in the fridge, he says.

14.30 Gurb takes a shower, sprays himself with perfume, does his hair, then puts on make-up. Gets me to call him a taxi. My goodness, always in such a hurry and always late wherever I go, he complains. What a life! Try to suggest that if he got up earlier and didn't burn the candle at both ends quite so much, he wouldn't get into such a state, but he has already rushed out. Have to pick up the clothes he has left strewn all over the place.

14.50 Nothing in the fridge apart from a half-empty bottle of champagne, a musty orchid and several test-tubes, the contents of which I prefer not to analyse.

15.00 Eat at the bar in Casa Vicente. Seasonal salad or gazpacho, chicken pasta, 650 pesetas. Bread, drinks, dessert and coffee on top. Including VAT and the tip, that comes to 900 altogether.

16.00 Return to Gurb's apartment. Thirty something messages on his machine. Listen to the first four. Sift through his letters: nothing but bills.

16.40 Two photo albums. Press cuttings: Gurb in Sa Tuna, Gurb in the Zarzuela Palace, Gurb at the bull running. A lopsided, blurred Polaroid: Gurb with a stranger on what might be a Paris street. Gurb going into Danielli's; coming out of Harry's Bar. Gurb as queen of this year's mining engineers' graduation ball. Hugging Yves Saint Laurent after a show. At a terrace on the Paseo de la Castellana with Mario Conde. Dancing with I. M. Pei and Partners. Breaking a bottle of champagne on the bow of the new torpedo boat *José María Pemán*. Shopping with Raissa in Saks Fifth Avenue: Mister Saks and Mister Fifth attending their famous clients: *Dear* ladies, *dear* ladies! Sponsor of the first (and last) rhinoceros born in Madrid Zoo. At a terrace on the Paseo de la Castellana with Captain Kirk and Doctor Spock. Dancing with Akbar Hashemi Rafsanjani.

17.08 Take myself to the corner supermarket. Food, cleaning products, wine, soft drinks, Kleenex. Total: 13,674 pesetas. Keep the bill to settle up with Gurb. Keep the numbers for the draw for a Honda Civic for myself.

17.30 Back at Gurb's apartment. Watch Los Mundos de Yupi.

18.00 Watch *Avanç, de l'informatiu vespre.*

18.30 Watch *Maritrapu eta mattinrapuren abenturak.* Then some video clips.

20.00 Put on water to boil. Add salt, then carrots, potatoes, cabbage, leeks, celery, a chicken wing, a meat bone. Look at my watch.

21.30 Switch off the stove. Lay the table. Water the plants on the terrace.

23.00 Late-night films. 'Chip off the Block' series. Tonight: *Son of Ben-Hur* (1931) with Ben Turpin and Olivia de Havilland. Next week ... *Son of Balarrasa* with José Sazatornil.

24.30 Brush my teeth; say my prayers and lie down on the sofa. No word from Gurb.

01.00 Can't get to sleep.

02.00 Can't get to sleep.

03.00 Can't get to sleep.

04.00 Get up. Pace up and down apartment to calm my nerves. Since I do not remember where all the furniture is, bang into the corner of everything with my shins.

04.20 Sit at the table. Pick up paper and felt-tip pen.

'Dear Gurb,
    It sometimes happens that two people can live together for a long while without really getting to know each other. The opposite may also sometimes be true – that is, that two people do not live together

for a long time and yet paradoxically get to know each other well. Or it may be that two people live together for a long time and one of them gets to know the other without that other person getting to know the first one, and in this case we cannot say that they have got to know each other, although at the same time we cannot say that neither of them knows the other. None of this, of course, has anything to do with us, and if I take the liberty of bringing it up, it is because I would not want you to think that I am seeking to introduce anything irrelevant to the matter at hand or not related to it. Furthermore, I am going to start this letter again, in part because of what I have just written, and in part because by now I have completely lost the thread.'

04.35 'Dear Gurb,
First, I should like to make a clear distinction between two fundamental concepts, that is between principles and precepts.'

04.50 'Dear Gurb,
Now that summer is almost here, I think it is time for us to leave.'

04.51 Stick the letter to the boudoir mirror with a drop of glue. Reread what I have written. Decide to take on the appearance of Yves Montand and sing mournfully:

Si vous avez peur
Des chagrins d'amour,
Evitez les belles …

The words do not sound quite as they should, since due to a mechanical problem I have taken on the appearance of Jacques-Yves Cousteau, and it's difficult to keep the tune in a diving suit.

05.05 Use my nail scissors to reduce Gurb's wardrobe to micro-organisms.

05.12 Tip the contents of all the perfume bottles down the sink, and fill them up again with sulphuric acid. Paint moustaches on all the pictures; fill the fridge with leeches; smear snot on the curtains; record farts on the answering machine; put a pig in the bath. Storm out of the apartment, slamming the door.

05.35 Go into the only bar in the neighbourhood that is still open. Numerous clientele, but as most of them are horizontal on the floor, there is plenty of room at the bar. Order six whiskies. Doubles.

06.35 Reach *my own* apartment. Collapse into my own bed and fall fast asleep even before my eyes are shut.

Day 24

09.12 Wake up with a blinding hangover, but pleased at the decision I've taken. Breakfast: churros with whisky. Temperature, 22º C; humidity, 68 per cent; skies cloudy with poor visibility on the coast; seas, choppy, wave height less than 1 metre. Perfect weather for my plans.

09.30 Leave my apartment. Stride purposefully down the staircase. If it moves, that's not my fault. Meet the caretaker hanging out her washing on the lift cables. Tell her I want to speak to her on a personal matter. Could I come to her cubbyhole?

09.31 Caretaker leads me to her cubbyhole, situated in the basement of the building. She shows it to me, and complains that in summer it's an oven, and in winter a fridge. She has no cooker, so is forced to grill her herrings on a camping gas stove. Then the smoke prevents her from seeing her TV. And she says she doesn't have a bathroom. Luckily, the building's pipes run through her bedroom, so whenever there is a leak she can have a shower. But, she adds, why should I care about any of this?

09.47 Reply that I have decided to take my leave of the city, and consequently am going to make her a present of my apartment. Hand over the deeds and the keys. The caretaker confides that she always knew I was a gentleman, not like others, who are all mouth and no trousers. To seal our friendship we both drink copiously from the bottle of whisky I've brought.

10.00 Appear at the front door of the chairman of the residents' association. Despite the importance of his position, he receives me in pyjamas. Inform him I intend to provide him with sufficient funds to get the crappy lift in the building replaced, paint the staircase, renew the facade, change all the pipe-work, repair the entry phone, seal the cracks on the roof, install a satellite dish and carpet the lobby. In return, I add, all I ask is to be remembered with affection, as I am about to embark on a long journey. The chairman says that if everybody were like me, there would be no need for all this socialism and other nonsense. We have a drink of whisky.

10.20 Appear at my neighbour's door. She opens it herself. She tells me she was about to go out, and that if it's all the same to me, could I come back later. I reply that there will be no later, because I too am about to go away, for an indefinite length of time. Might I come in? It will only take a minute. She agrees somewhat reluctantly, because by this time I must stink something rotten of whisky.

10.30 As delicately as I can, I tell my neighbour that I have been so bold as to investigate her emotional and economic circumstances, and that both of them could best be described as disastrous. I add that as regards emotions, I have nothing to offer, because I have no time left at all. But as for the economic side …

10.35 Clear my throat. Pluck up my courage with another few sips of whisky. Continue.

10.36 … as for the economic side, I say, since I am single, a man of property and generous by nature, I have decided, if she has nothing against the idea, to deposit in a (Swiss) bank sufficient funds to pay for her son's education both here and now and in the future at the Harvard School of Business Administration. And as regards herself, I add in a faint voice, I beg her in memory of the short time we spent as neighbours, to accept this modest emerald necklace.

10.39 Present the necklace to my neighbour, polish off the bottle of whisky, rush out of her apartment and roll down the stairs.

12.00 Walk from the metro station back to the space-ship. When I arrive my heart sinks. Ivy has covered all the hatches, the paint has come off in various places, someone has torn off the Sacred Heart on the door. I can't show myself back on my planet in a state like this.

12.02 In the village, buy a scourer, Vim cleaning pow-der and a pair of rubber gloves. Return to the ship and set to work like billy-o.

13.30 Enter the spaceship. Apart from a few patches of damp, the interior does not appear to have suffered any major damage. Check the gauges, the fuel. Every-thing normal. Sit at the controls. Ignite the engines ... vroom ... vroom ... vroom ...

13.45 Vroom ... vroom ... vroom ...

14.00 Vroom ... vroom ... vroom ...

14.20 VRROOMM!

14.21 Jesus, what a fright.

14.22 Switch off engine. Go back down into the vil-lage to buy provisions.

15.00 Load the ship with all I need to make the journey more bearable: toothpaste, the latest books, a bicycle, a summary of the problems concerning the metro in Montjuich and little else.

16.00 Just when I've filled the hold with provisions, notice that the ship has been overrun by cockroaches. What can I do? I could buy lots of cans of Baygon, but once I've returned to my state of pure intellect, how would I press the button on the top?

16.20 After several attempts, succeed in getting in touch with Space Station AF in the constellation of Antares. Inform them that I am concluding my mission on Earth and am about to return, taking advantage of the poor atmospheric conditions (ideal for navigation). At the same time, inform them that I am returning alone, because my colleague on the expedition, Gurb by name, has gone missing while on active duty. Avoid telling the truth in order not to upset his aged parents.

16.30 Space Station AF in the constellation of Antares asks me to repeat the message. Apparently they are having problems with reception.

16.40 Repeat the message. The crew of Space Station AF in the constellation of Antares admits they heard it perfectly well the first time, but wanted me to repeat it because they thought my Catalan accent was a hoot.

17.00 Appear at señora Mercedes and señor Joaquín's bar. Señora Mercedes is behind the counter as ever. Señor Joaquín is playing dominoes with three locals of his own age. Warm greetings, aubergine omelette, glass of beer. Tell them I've come to say goodbye. I'm going back to my own world. See, Joaquín? I always said the gentleman wasn't from around here. Give them the present I have bought for them: a small house and 11 acres of land in Florida, where they can go and have a rest. Oh, but you shouldn't have. That must have cost you an arm and a leg. Don't say that, señora Mercedes, you deserve it and much more besides. Farwell, farewell. Send us a postcard.

19.00 Everything ready for take-off. Airlocks closed. Start the countdown: 100, 99, 98, 97 …

19.01 A noise behind me. Could it be those blasted cockroaches? Go and look.

19.02 Gurb! What on earth are you doing here? And with those platform heels! Do you think that is any way to travel through space (or time)? Gurb points to a coded message on the instrument panel.

19.05 Decipher the message. It is from the Supreme Junta. In view of the success of our mission on Earth (for which they congratulate us) we are to change course and head (with the same objective) for the planet BWR 143, which spins (like an idiot) around Alpha Centauri. On arrival, just as we have done on Earth, we are to adopt the appearance of the planet's inhabitants. They have forty-nine legs, of which only two reach the ground; they also have one eye, six ears, eight noses and eleven tiny teeth. They eat mud and some hairy caterpillars they catch by means of their penultimate pair of tentacles.

19.07 From Gurb's sulky expression, deduce that the mission we have been entrusted with does not fill him with a just sense of pride. Before he can express his lack of enthusiasm in a way which might force me to take disciplinary measures, I try to convince him with a variety of arguments, which could be grouped into three (or fewer) categories, namely: a) the relevant authorities always know what is good for us better than we do, b) travelling to new places and learning about other cultures is always instructive, and c) he who pays the piper pays the tune. On a more personal note, I add that, in his particular case, the change will do him the world of good, because lately he's become a bit soft in the head and it's high time he forgot about being a beautiful, rich and lively young woman and turned into a disgusting worm. Gurb replies by saying that he does not know what he admires more: my perspicacity or my ability to make myself clear.

19.50 Lift-off achieved without problems at the appointed time (983674856739 hours on the cosmic astrolabe). Take-off speed: 0.12 on the conventional (restricted) scale. Angle of incidence relative to perihelion: 54 degrees. Forecast length of voyage: 784 years. Destination: ALPHA CENTAURI.

19.55 Gurb and I emerge from behind advertising hoarding, slightly scorched by the blowback from the ship's engines. We watch the craft disappear through the clouds. We have to hurry if we don't want to get caught out by rain before we reach the metro.

20.00 Gurb expresses the view (erroneous, in my opinion) that I am an idiot. If I hadn't spent my last cent giving all and sundry presents just to show off, he says, we could now call a taxi and save ourselves the walk. He adds that he finds it really difficult walking in his tube dress. In future, he says, he'll take care of money matters. Before I can remind him that although we are outside the spaceship (and the law), I am still his superior officer, a car goes by. Gurb waves his arms and it stops. Gurb pulls up his skirt and runs after it. Ignoring my shouts of command, he gets in. The car pulls off.

02.00 No word from Gurb.